FIGHTING FANTASY

RETURN TO
FIRETOP
MOUNTAIN

IAN
LIVINGSTONE

SCHOLASTIC

Published in the UK by Scholastic Children's Books, 2020
Euston House, 24 Eversholt Street, London, NW1 1DB, UK
A division of Scholastic Limited.

London – New York – Toronto – Sydney – Auckland
Mexico City – New Delhi – Hong Kong

SCHOLASTIC and associated logos are trademarks and/or
registered trademarks of Scholastic Inc.

First published in the UK by Penguin Group, 1992

Text © Ian Livingstone, 1992
Illustration copyright © Martin McKenna, 1992
Cover and map illustration copyright © Ian Livingstone, 2020

The right of Ian Livingstone and Martin McKenna to be identified
as the author and illustrator of this work has been asserted by
them under the Copyright, Designs and Patents Act 1988.

Cover illustration by Robert Ball, 2020
Map illustration by Leo Hartas, 2017

Fighting Fantasy is a trademark owned by Steve Jackson
and Ian Livingstone, all rights reserved.
Fighting Fantasy Gamebook Concept © Steve Jackson and Ian Livingstone, 1982

ISBN 978 0702 30571 9

Printed by CPI Group (UK) Ltd, Croydon, CR0 4YY
Papers used by Scholastic Children's Books are made
from wood grown in sustainable forests.

1 3 5 7 9 10 8 6 4 2

www.scholastic.co.uk

Official FIGHTING FANTASY website: www.fightingfantasy.com

CONTENTS

HOW WILL YOU START
YOU ADVENTURE?

The book you hold in your hands is a gateway to another world – a world of dark magic, terrifying monsters, brooding castles, treacherous dungeons and untold danger, where a noble few defend against the myriad schemes of the forces of evil. Welcome to the world of **FIGHTING FANTASY**!

You are about to embark upon a thrilling fantasy adventure in which **YOU** are the hero! **YOU** decide which route to take, which dangers to risk and which creatures to fight. But be warned – it will also be **YOU** who has to live or die by the consequences of your actions.

Take heed, for success is by no means certain, and you may well fail in your mission on your first attempt.

But have no fear, for with experience, skill and luck, each new attempt should bring you a step closer to your ultimate goal.

Prepare yourself, for when you turn the page you will enter an exciting, perilous **FIGHTING FANTASY** adventure where every choice is yours to make, an adventure in which **YOU ARE THE HERO**!

How would you like to begin your adventure?

IF YOU ARE NEW TO FIGHTING FANTASY...

It's a good idea to read through the rules which appear on pages 239-245 before you start.

IF YOU HAVE PLAYED FIGHTING FANTASY BEFORE...

You'll realize that to have any chance of success, you will need to discover your hero's attributes. You can create your own character by following the instructions on pages 239–240. Don't forget to enter your character's details on the Adventure Sheet which appears on page 246.

Also note that, unlike other Fighting Fantasy Gamebooks, in this adventure you do not start with any Provisions.

ALTERNATIVE DICE

If you do not have a pair of dice handy, dice rolls are printed throughout the book at the bottom of the pages. Flicking rapidly through the book and stopping on a page will give you a random dice roll. If you need to 'roll' only one die, read only the first printed die; if two, total the two dice symbols.

BACKGROUND

Ten years is not a long time in a wizard's life – some live for over two hundred years, keeping themselves alive by their own magic and potions. There is a well-known saying among wizards which goes: 'You're a long time dead, so let's live instead!' Some wizards even went one step further: they cast a spell on themselves so that, in the event of their being slain or assassinated, they were able to raise themselves after a predetermined time when their assailant was long gone. The wizards who chose to come back from the dead were, however, always aligned to evil, for it was dark magic that was needed to cheat death. One of those wizards was known (and feared) by the name of Zagor, the infamous Warlock of Firetop Mountain. Ten years have passed since the day when he was killed by a brave adventurer who risked the guards and deadly traps deep inside Firetop Mountain to save Allansia from his evil magic. But killing Zagor is one thing; keeping him dead is another. Nobody knew that Zagor had cast the Raise Dead Spell on himself, otherwise the adventurer who killed him would have sealed him inside his mountain tomb.

But all that was ten years ago. In the last six months, sinister events have begun to happen around Firetop Mountain. First, the top of the mountain, which was famous for its red-coloured bracken, has turned deathly black. Livestock which have grazed on and around the mountain for decades have started to die a sickening death, and recently people have even disappeared, dragged inside the mountain (it is said) by hideous creatures of the night. Those good people who remain are terrified, for it is rumoured that Zagor has risen and is building himself a new body, bit by bit, from the unfortunate villagers of Anvil!

You are an adventurer, a sword for hire, wandering through the lands. Coming to the village of Anvil, you decide to stop for a rest after your week-long march. However, as soon as you enter the village you sense that all is not well. The villagers look frightened and women quickly push their children indoors as you walk along the main street. You decide that the local tavern would be the best place to find out what is troubling the villagers, so you enter the Two Moons. The chatter inside dies down quickly to a low murmur and the customers eye you as you walk up to the bar. The barman stares at you sternly, and you can see by the look in his eyes that he is a proud man trying to hide his fear.

'Yes?' he grunts in a low voice.

You tell him that you are an adventurer seeking a new quest that will end in riches and honour. He frowns, not knowing whether to trust you.

'Does the name Zagor mean anything to you?' he asks softly, watching you closely for a reaction.

'Zagor,' you reply confidently, 'was the Warlock of Firetop Mountain until he was slain, ten years ago.'

'*Is* the Warlock of Firetop Mountain,' the barman says dramatically. 'He's come back to life! He is building himself a new body and is sending his evil servants to Anvil to take back live donors!'

The barman seems to accept you as a friend and quickly goes on to tell you about the doom that has befallen Anvil, thanks to Zagor.

'We need help, stranger!' he says desperately. 'None of us here has the power to defeat Zagor ... but maybe you do. We are poor and cannot pay you what you deserve to take on such a task, but we do know that there are chests full of gold inside Firetop Mountain. Will you help us?'

By now the tavern is silent. All eyes are upon you. How can you let them down? Slowly you smile and nod your head.

'On one condition,' you say.

'Name it,' the barman replies.

'That I get a hot bath and a room for the night!' you laugh.

'Done!'

Everyone in the tavern lets out a cheer, and they all gather round to slap you on the back and offer to buy you some ale.

In the morning you find the barman, whose name you learn is Moose, cooking a large breakfast for you.

'You must set off south immediately to visit the grand wizard Yaztromo. He alone can prepare you for such an adversary as Zagor. Don't even think about tackling

Zagor on your own. He is stronger than ever and his magic is deadly,' Moose says earnestly.

You thank him for his advice and bid him farewell.

Now turn to paragraph 1.

YOUR ADVENTURE AWAITS!

May your STAMINA never fail!

NOW TURN OVER...

'Quick, follow me, we must catch them.'

1

Leaving Anvil and its villagers behind, you set off east deep in thought. Firetop Mountain is only a short distance from Anvil, but to go all the way to Yaztromo's Tower first would mean losing many days' valuable time. How could Yaztromo help? Ever since he single-handedly defeated eight ghoulish Dark Elves on the edge of Darkwood Forest, the place where he built his famous tower, his reputation has grown. Wise, good, powerful, philanthropic and many other words were used to describe the great Yaztromo. Many sought his help against evil and none were turned away. Suddenly there is a shout from behind you. You spin around, to see Moose running towards you. You notice that his sword is drawn and there is a look of alarm on his face.

'Zagor will know of your plan unless we can catch the two Trackers I saw running from Anvil, a few minutes ago. They must have overheard us and are running back to inform Zagor. Quick, follow, me, we must catch them,' Moose says hurriedly, still panting. He runs off into the undergrowth, shouting at you to follow him. If you wish to do so, turn to **341**. If you would rather continue to walk along the path alone, turn to **161**.

2

Now the undead Chaos Warrior can be defeated only by piercing its heart. As it lumbers towards you with its great sword outstretched, you try an upward thrust with your sword in order to strike under its breastplate.

UNDEAD CHAOS WARRIOR   *SKILL 10*   *STAMINA 0*

If you win an Attack Round, the Chaos Warrior does not lose STAMINA points. Instead, you must roll one die: a roll of 1–4 means that you missed its heart; a roll of 5 or 6 means that your blow pierced its heart and kills it. If you win, turn to **88**.

3

On turning the corner, you come across an old wooden bench above which there is a sign, but the painted words on the sign have all but flaked off. All you can make out is the first word, which is 'Rest'. If you want to sit down on the bench, turn to **211**. If you would rather walk on, turn to **162**.

4

It is not long before you arrive at a great iron door in the right-hand wall. The door is firmly locked, but there is a large keyhole in the door. If you have an iron key, turn to the paragraph number that is inscribed on the key. If you do not have an iron key, you will have to walk on (turn to **172**).

5

As you lean over the rack and reach for the skeleton's finger, you hear a smothered laugh coming from above. Looking up, you see a weighted net dropping down on top of you. Roll two dice. If the total is less than or equal to your SKILL, turn to **339**. If the total is greater than your SKILL, turn to **252**.

6

Not wishing to draw attention to yourself, you tell the Barbarian that you will be back later to deal with him. You gulp down a mug of water to get rid of the taste of the eyeballs and now, although you are bloated, at least you have eaten. Regain 1 STAMINA point. You walk past the Lizard Men guards and turn right into the tunnel (turn to **304**).

7

You wait for a gap to appear between the worms on the floor, then you jump. The Sucker Worms show no interest in you, preferring to feast on the dead flesh of the dog. However, one of the worms has rolled over on top of the box. Will you wait for it to slide off the box (turn to **307**) or hack at it with your sword straight away (turn to **396**)?

8

As soon as you touch the wizard's hand, he starts to laugh out loud. His body starts to shimmer and soon you are able to see right through him; this is because you are shaking the hand of a doppelganger, not the hand of Yaztromo. The ghost-like figure has the ability to drain you of your life; when you look down, you see that your own body is turning transparent too. You try to pull your hand away but it is too late. You are doomed to live in a twilight world forever. Your adventure is over.

9

Coming from above you hear the sound of hands clapping, and look up to see the Pitmaster smiling. He drops a rope down to you and you climb up out of the pit. He leads you over to the second pit, saying, 'Your next opponent has cunning and deception as well as strength. The Metallix is not what it seems.'

You look down into the pit and discover a sinewy-looking creature, no more than a metre tall. With its large, soulful eyes and drooping mouth it looks almost harmless. Remembering the Pitmaster's warning, however, you jump down into the pit, sword in hand. The Metallix does not flinch and appears almost unconcerned by your arrival. You walk towards the Metallix – and still it doesn't move. You raise your sword above your head, ready to strike. But then it crosses your mind that perhaps the Metallix *wants* you to strike it. If you want to try to cut off its head, turn to **195**. If you would rather pick a rock up off the floor and throw it at the beast to get it to move, turn to **279**.

10

You know you will have only a few minutes to escape before the Mummies come back to life. Spying the door at the end of the hallway, you make a quick exit (turn to **102**).

11

As the morning wears on, dark clouds appear overhead and the wind quickly picks up. The unstable boat is caught by a sudden gust and tilts disconcertingly over to one side. If the crew consists of five or fewer members (including yourself), turn to **54**. If there are more than five crew left on board, turn to **312**.

12

You place your treasure in your backpack, unaware that one of the diamonds has been treated with evil magic; it is likely that sooner or later you will meet an untimely death. For now, you must choose which way to go: if you want to enter the left-hand tunnel, turn to **124**; if you prefer to enter the right-hand tunnel, turn to **38**.

The battle rages for some minutes

13

You soon come to another door, but this time there is no window to look through. You press your ear to the door and hear what sounds like somebody moaning in pain. If you want to open the door, turn to **118**. If you would rather walk on, turn to **387**.

14

You whip the dagger out of your boot and throw it at the rat. At such short range you can hardly miss, and you skewer it to the floor. The piece of tooth rolls on to the floor just in time to release the Fire Elemental, as the massive Earth Elemental is descending on you. The Fire Elemental wraps its fiery arm round the waist of the Earth Elemental and tries to lift it off the ground; at the same time it is being pounded by gigantic stone fists. The battle rages for some minutes, until finally the Earth Elemental crumbles into a heap of broken boulders and scorched earth. The flame dies and you look up to the throne where Zagor sits, looking ill-at-ease.

He begins to chant again. He has decided to copy you, and suddenly a jet of flame shoots out of the floor at the bottom of the steps. Another fiery humanoid has been summoned, a Fire Elemental, the last of his Elementals of Chaos. If you have one more golden dragon's tooth, you must throw it on the floor to defend yourself against the demon fire. If you have the right tooth, turn to the paragraph which has the same number as the one on the tooth. If you do not have the tooth, turn to **365**.

<h3 style="text-align:center">15</h3>

With not a moment to spare, you take the garlic out of your backpack and thrust it out in front of you to halt the Gorgon ... but garlic is useful only against the Undead; it is useless against a creature like a Gorgon. Transfixed by fear, you stare blankly at the monster towering above you. Turn to **265**.

<h3 style="text-align:center">16</h3>

The acid continues to burn – but there is nothing you can do about it. It burns right through your cheek, enters your mouth and starts to trickle down your throat. No amount of coughing and spitting can save you. Your adventure is over.

<h3 style="text-align:center">17</h3>

With lightning speed you clutch at your throat and manage to tear the rat away before it is able to wound you. You fling it to the floor then bring the heel of your boot down hard on top of it, crushing it out of shape. Cursing the Goblins, you leave the cellar and walk back to the path in order to continue south (turn to **238**).

18

You discover many strange titles on the book shelves: *Casket of Souls, Transmutation, The Dark Light* and *Vampire Blood* are just a few, but the one that catches your attention is a tiny leather-bound book entitled *Eye of the Dragon.* You open it at random, but the print is too small to read. If you have a magnifying glass and wish to read the book, turn to **53**. If you would rather read *Vampire Blood,* turn to **290**.

19

Among boulders set back some thirty metres from the path, you see a drawing roughly daubed in white paint on a small rock. If you want to take a closer look at the drawing, turn to **171**. If you would rather press on towards Firetop Mountain, turn to **64**.

20

The staff is made of polished hawthorn, with a skull carved from bone fixed on top; you decide to take it with you. If you haven't done so already, you may take the lid off the basket (turn to **107**). Otherwise, there is nothing for you to do except to pursue the Death Lords (turn to **219**).

21

You fill the bucket with straw from the bed and set it on fire, using the torch that is set in the wall. As the smoke begins to fill the cell and stream out between the cell door bars, you start shouting. You hear the Goblin curse and stand by the side of the door, ready to leap on the Goblin if it falls for your trick. To find out how stupid the Goblin is, roll two dice. If the total rolled is 7 or less, turn to **207**. If the total is 8-12, turn to **343**.

22

You quickly take the bell out of your backpack and shake it vigorously. A magical note rings out and the witch covers her ears, trying to shut out the pure sound. She staggers backwards and starts to scream, before collapsing to the floor, unconscious. The Dog Beast appears unharmed by the bell's ringing. It drops the bowl it is carrying and charges at you, swinging a ball and chain.

MUTANT DOG BEAST   SKILL 8   STAMINA 8

If you win, turn to **282**.

23

You come to the end of the tunnel, where it joins a cross-tunnel. An iron portcullis blocks your way and it is far too heavy to lift. On the wall to your right are two levers. On closer inspection you see that the left-hand one is a dummy made out of old black wax – a trap laid many years ago. You decide to pull the other lever. Slowly and noisily the portcullis rises into the ceiling and you walk safely under it. Looking to the left, you see that the tunnel ends at the mass of rubble of a cave-in. Looking right, the tunnel continues for thirty metres before bearing left. If you want to go to the left to the end of the tunnel, turn to **308**. If you want to go right, turn to **3**.

24

The box contains bits and pieces that the Chaos Warrior must have collected over the years. Among the items you find a rat's skull, a copper bracelet, 3 Gold pieces, 2 Silver Pieces, a page from a tiny book, a horseshoe, a calling horn, and a silver pendant on a beaded cord. You put them all into your backpack except the page from the book, the copper bracelet and the silver pendant. Will you now:

Read the page from the book?	Turn to **322**
Put the copper bracelet on your wrist?	Turn to **62**
Hang the pendant round your neck?	Turn to **105**
Put the bracelet and the pendant in	

your backpack?	Turn to **313**
Take a look at the weapons, if you have not done so already?	Turn to **206**
Leave the room and walk on up the tunnel?	Turn to **151**

25

Although in pain, you fight blindly on, swinging your sword from side to side.

GORGON SKILL 10 STAMINA 8

Each time you lose an Attack Round, you will also suffer bites from the Gorgon's snakes. Roll one die and deduct that number of points from your STAMINA. If you win, turn to **79**.

26

You take the article out of your backpack and hand it to the Troglodyte, who examines it with a smile on his face. (Remove the item from your *Equipment List*.) You explain to the Troglodyte that, regrettably, you do not have time to stay and watch the competition, but he is too engrossed in admiration of the prize to hear you as you slip quietly out of the room and turn right along the tunnel (turn to **304**).

27

You drop the tooth on the floor and watch it break in two. A fountain of water shoots up out of the floor and rises, forming into the shape of a liquid Titan. Suddenly it flows forward and crashes down on top of the Fire Elemental in a giant cloud of steam. The Water Elemental hisses loudly as it battles with the flames. For a moment it looks as if the Water Elemental will boil away to nothing, but gradually the flames die down and go out. Quiet returns to the hall as the Water Elemental retreats to the tooth. When the steam clears, you see Zagor standing at the base of the steps. He looks shaken and stands with his head a little down. Perhaps his magic power is all but spent?

'We will finish this battle with a duel,' he says solemnly. 'We will fight with long knives and wearing no armour. Accept this challenge or with my last energies I will crush you with a thunderbolt. We are equals, you and I, and we must fight on equal terms. It is the struggle between Chaos and Order we must decide. If I win, Chaos will swallow Allansia. If I lose, Order will return. Prepare to die! Chaos awaits Allansia!' Zagor removes his robes and stands, bare chested, before you. Ugly red scars cover his body as a result of the many transplants he has recently received. The skeletal stump that is his left arm protrudes awkwardly from his shoulder. You shudder at the sight of him; you know you must accept his challenge, so you

The Fire Sprite leaps out of the fire

remove your armour. Zagor throws you a knife and walks slowly towards you. The fate of Allansia rests on this final battle.

ZAGOR   SKILL *11*   STAMINA *18*

If you win, turn to **400**.

28

After gathering some wood, you soon have a fire burning. You settle back against the boulder and are soon fast asleep. Unknown to you, however, the wood has been left there on purpose by one of Zagor's servants. The flames start to jump about and then take on the shape of a small, human-shaped being. The Fire Sprite leaps out of the fire and grabs your outstretched arms. Deduct 3 points from your STAMINA. YOU awake in pain, trying desperately to shake the Fire Sprite off your arm, but it does not loosen its flaming grip. Will you attack it with your sword (turn to **193**) or try to smother it with your blanket (turn to **98**)?

29

'So!' shouts the hunchback, 'you are in the employ of Zagor, are you? Well, any servant of Zagor is an enemy of mine.' Before you have time to explain, the old man hits you across the back with his crooked stick. This is no ordinary stick, however, but a withering stick! The blow in itself is not too painful, but your back seems to bend and contract, quickly stiffening and locking in its new position, and you find yourself unable to stand up straight. Deduct 2 points from your SKILL. You draw your sword and shout at the old man to undo the damage he has done you.

'Come another step closer and I'll whack you again, you evil leech!' the hunchback shouts back. If you wish to attack the old man, turn to **205**. If you would rather try to reason with him again, turn to **301**.

30

The ring you are wearing allows you to see through illusions. The image of the woman and the young boy slowly fade away, revealing their true identities. In front of you stands a hideous-looking hunchbacked witch. Her wiry, bent and hairy fingers end in long, dirty nails. Her eyes are dark and hollow and her clothes are tattered rags. Her servant is a mutant beast with a human torso and a dog's head. All at once you hear a voice inside your head, a warning from the ring, crying out, 'Ring the bell! Ring the bell!'

If you are carrying a silver bell, turn to **22**. If you are not carrying a bell, turn to **228**.

31

You turn your head away before the hideous creature can look you in the eyes, knowing that catching her glance for just a second will be enough to turn you to stone. You must act quickly to defeat her. Will you attack her with your sword, with your free hand covering your eyes (turn to **393**), or search your backpack for an item to use against her (turn to **66**)?

32

You soon arrive at another door, this time in the right-hand wall of the tunnel. If you want to open the door, turn to **144**. If you would rather walk on, turn to **97**.

33

You prise the lid off the box with the tip of your sword, and you discover a small leather pouch inside. The pouch contains a small wooden ball and a small wooden brick. Deciding to keep them, you put them in your pocket. If you have not done so already, you may now examine the clay pots (turn to **386**) or go to sleep (turn to **95**). If you would rather find somewhere else to sleep, turn to **180**.

34

You whip the dagger out of your boot and throw it at the Goblin. Roll two dice. If the total is less than or equal to your SKILL, turn to **371**. If the total is greater than your SKILL, turn to **130**.

35

The daggers held in the tight grip of the Death Head stop glowing and turn black. You decide against picking them up. If you have not done so already, you may now smash the red pot (turn to **41**). Otherwise, there is nothing for you to do except walk over to the new door in the other room (turn to **347**).

36

'So, you must indeed be a friend,' Zoot says excitedly. 'Alas, I will not be able to recognize you. While I was flying back to Kaad on my giant eagle, a Fire Dragon attacked. I was blinded and my beautiful eagle was badly burnt. We crash-landed in some trees. The eagle in her last heroic moment saved my life but gave up her own, trying to shield me. An Orc patrol picked me up and brought me here, gleefully telling me that my left arm was to be sewn on to Zagor in place of his own rotten bones. Set me free and I'll help you defeat this evil warlock.' You prise open his iron shackles and help him to his feet. 'I may be blind but I'm still a Half-Elf. My sense of touch may well prove useful in this trap-infested hell-hole. Let's go.'

You lead Zoot out of the room and turn right along the tunnel which ends, however, at a stone wall. There are footprints on the floor, which all point towards the end wall. You tell Zoot that you think there may be a secret door in the wall. He runs his fingers slowly over the wall, searching for hairline cracks. He soon finds a loose stone and carefully pulls it out. There is an iron handle in the recess.

'This handle will open the secret door, but I think there's a hidden trap attached to it. There may be another way of opening the door.' At the foot of the wall he finds another loose stone with another handle behind it. 'This will be the one, I'm sure. Hello, I've found something else. Here, take a look and tell me what it is.'

It is a large tooth made of solid gold which has the number '186' stamped on it. Add 1 point to your LUCK.

Zoot smiles when you describe it to him. 'Stand back while I turn this handle. You never know, I've been wrong before.'

He turns the handle and you hear a click. The secret door swings open inwards – but at the same time the floor stone on which Zoot is standing drops away beneath him. You hear his loud scream fade away as he falls to his death at the bottom of a spiked pit. Spurred on by sudden anger, you leap across the pit and through the doorway, landing safely in a cross-tunnel. The secret door swings slowly back and slams shut, and now you cannot even tell that it is there.

Looking to the left, you see an iron portcullis in the left-hand wall of the tunnel which goes on for another twenty metres before ending at the mass of rubble of a cave-in. Looking right, the tunnel continues for twenty metres before turning left. If you want to take a look at the portcullis, turn to **253**. If you would rather go to the right, turn to **3**.

37

A few metres up the tunnel you see three doors in the right-hand wall. You walk up to the first door and press your ear against it, but you can hear nothing. The handle turns in your hand. Will you open the door (turn to **389**) or walk on to the second door (turn to **56**)?

38

You step warily into the torchlit tunnel. In the distance you can see that the tunnel opens out into another cavern, lined with bookshelves that are crammed with hundreds of books. Standing in the middle of the cavern is a black-robed person whose folded arms are concealed in baggy sleeves which almost touch the floor. A large black hood completely covers the figure's lead.

'Enter, stranger,' a deep voice calls. 'You have chosen the path of the Puzzles. I am the Inquisitor. It is your task to prove to me that you are worthy to pass through my domain, and only by the power of your mind shall you do so. Fail, and you shall die. Step forward and listen carefully, your test begins.'

If you want to obey the Inquisitor, turn to **262**. If you would rather attack him, turn to **141**.

39

There is just a single sentence on the page; it reads: *The Water Elemental of Light is numbered 27 and destroys the Fire Elemental of Chaos.* You memorize the words while you walk on up the tunnel (turn to **97**).

40

A white dove circles then lands on the deck, and you notice that a small pouch is attached to its leg. The bird appears to be unconcerned as you untie the pouch from its leg. Inside you find a message from Moose: 'Zagor has sent a doppelganger, a ghost-like impostor of Yaztromo, to trap you when you reach Kaad. But, as you know, doppelgangers always have green eyes and Yaztromo's eyes are blue. Beware!' Wondering how Zagor has found out about your mission, you throw the message into the river. The dove flies off as the boat continues its rapid journey downstream. Turn to **11**.

41

You drop the pot on the floor and watch it shatter into dozens of pieces. Lying among the debris of the shattered pot you see a round, black stone. If you want to pick it up, turn to **154**. Alternatively, if you have not done so already, you may smash the brown pot (turn to **397**). If both pots are broken, you will have to return to the room containing the statues and try the new door there (turn to **347**).

The diamond transforms into a large warrior

42

One of the diamonds in your hand has been coated with a magic potion of Zagor's creation. The diamond immediately transforms into a large warrior constructed of diamonds. It raises its crystal sword and strikes at you.

DIAMOND SENTINEL   *SKILL* 11   *STAMINA* 9

The Sentinel cannot be harmed by edged weapons, so your sword is useless against it. Unless you have a hammer, you will soon be defeated and your adventure will be over. If you win using a hammer, turn to **63**.

43

You are conducted to a table, set up in the middle of a large room, around which three contestants are sitting, each with a plate of sheep's eyeballs piled high in front of him. You sit down to join them and gulp at the sight of the eyeballs in front of you. You look at the others and try to raise a smile. Your opponent to the left is an old Barbarian wearing furs and a leather headband. The one to your right is a neanderthal-looking caveman and the one sitting opposite you is another Troglodyte who, although of small build, has a pot belly . . . and everybody knows that sheep's eyes are a Troglodyte delicacy. The Barbarian looks at you fiercely and asks in a gruff voice, 'Do you want a side bet on this?'

If you want to have a bet with the Barbarian on the outcome of the competition, turn to **268**. If you don't want to bet, turn to **380**.

44

Ignoring the boy's request, you try the door of the store but find that it is locked. Thinking that you may come back later, you set off to find Zoot Zimmer. Turn to **309**.

45

As you creep over towards the sleeping Troglodyte, you tumble and trip over the rough floor. *Test your Luck.* If you are Lucky, turn to **70**. If you are Unlucky, turn to **191**.

46

The chasm is only a metre wide, but you are unable to jump across it: you hit an invisible wall in mid-air and stumble headlong down into the black void. You land on your back with a thump on a stone floor. Slowly the chasm above you closes up and you are left in total darkness. It is not long before you lose consciousness.

When you reawaken, you find yourself on a marble table and two Death Lords are hovering over you with sharp knives. 'Begin!' a voice shouts. In less than an hour Zagor will have a new limb – yours! Your adventure is over.

47

You take a couple of steps back, then run forward and jump as far as you can over the skulls. Roll two dice. If the total is less than or equal to your SKILL, turn to **168**. If the total is greater than your SKILL, turn to **261**.

48

The tunnel ends at a wooden door with many strange symbols carved on it. Various objects are nailed to the door, including old coins, a rabbit's foot, various small skulls, a copper triangle and a shrivelled ear. You listen at the door and hear a woman's voice ordering someone to bring her a bowl of crushed maggots. If you want to open the door, turn to **305**. If you want to turn back and go past the last junction, turn to **4**.

49

Reacting swiftly you fling your shield up to block the steel dagger, which clatters off the shield and falls harmlessly to the ground. You pick it up then charge into the bushes, brandishing your sword. Turn to **72**.

50

The sword and dagger disappear from the Inquisitor's bands. He folds his arms again slowly and says, 'Correct. Now for the second puzzle. You must tell me my age from the information I shall give you. I first went to the School of Evil Magic when I was 4½ years of age and I stayed there for a sixth of my life. Then I went to the School of Demonic Sorcery for a fifth of my life. I then studied under the great necromancer Hellmoon for a quarter of my life and, since then, for a third of my life I have been in the service of Zagor.'

If you can work out the Inquisitor's age, turn to the paragraph with that number. If you do not know the answer, turn to **127**.

51

You climb up through the hole in the ceiling into a small, candelit room with stone walls and a low roof, too low to allow you to stand upright. There is a narrow tunnel in one of the walls. A large sword hangs on the wall next to the tunnel entrance; its blade is made of a dark, almost black metal. If you wish to take the sword, turn to **355**. If you would rather squeeze through the narrow tunnel, turn to **68**.

52

'Very good,' the old man says calmly. 'You will make an excellent spy for Zagor, after I have made a few alterations to your mind. It is a simple task to alter the human brain for a Mindbender such as I. Now, should I change you into a servant of Chaos or make you just plain evil?' While the Mindbender is chuckling to himself, you decide to strike. Will you use:

A whip (if you have one)?	Turn to **382**
Garlic?	Turn to **224**
Your sword?	Turn to **174**

53

You turn to the chapter called 'Dragons' Teeth' and scan the page with the magnifying glass until you reach a section on 'The Elementals of Light and Chaos'. You read that there are four of each, the Supreme Elementals of Light appearing in the form of golden dragons' teeth. Each one is numbered. *The Air Elemental of Light is number 186 and destroys a Water Elemental of Chaos. The Earth Elemental of Light is* ... But the next three pages are missing from the book and you do not learn the secrets of the other Elementals. You memorize the information about the Air Elemental before walking through the cavern and into the tunnel at the far end (turn to **337**).

54

The crew try frantically to ease the sails and balance the boat, but the wind is too strong. The boat flips over on to its side, spilling you and the crew into the cold water. Roll one die; this is the number of Razorfish that converge and attack you without warning. If there are as many (or more) Razorfish as there are crew, including yourself, turn to **101**. If there are fewer Razorfish than there are crew, turn to **325**.

55

The dragons' teeth in the palm of your hand begin to feel warm, raising your spirits, as the Air Elemental starts to envelop you. The noise of the wind is deafening. You must cast one of the teeth on the floor immediately. If you know which one to use, turn to the paragraph which has the same number as the number on the tooth. If you do not have the tooth or do not have the right one to counter the Air Elemental, turn to **365**.

56

You listen intently at the door, but you can hear no sounds coming from the other side. You turn the handle and find that the door is unlocked. If you want to enter the room, turn to **226**. If you would rather walk on to the third door, turn to **273**.

57

'That is indeed my name, stranger, but how did you know it? Have we met somewhere before? Before I can trust you, I need to be convinced that you do know me. Can you tell me the number of my house in Hobnail Street?' If you know the number of the house, turn to the paragraph with that number. If you do not, turn to **176**.

58

You examine the dragon game pieces and find that they are carved out of wood and have been painted gold and silver. A search of the Skeletons yields 1 Gold Piece and a hollow glass ball which contains white smoke that swirls around inside as you rotate the ball. If you wish to smash the glass ball on the ground, turn to **392**. If you prefer to leave the ball in the room and re-enter the tunnel, turn to **373**.

59

Unknown to you, the silver rat is a charm which was made by Zagor – and contact with the human skin activates it! As soon as you put it round your neck, the small rat comes to life and starts to gnaw frantically at your throat. Roll two dice. If the total is less than or equal to your SKILL score, turn to **17**. If the total is greater than your SKILL score, turn to **276**.

One of the teeth in the dragon's jaw sparkles

60

Opening the door, you see a hunched, pock-marked creature wearing tattered grey rags and staggering under the weight of a dragon's skull which it is carrying across a filthy room. One of the teeth in the dragon's jaw sparkles; it could be made of gold. There is a large wooden crate at the back of the room, filled with straw, towards which the creature is walking. If you want to attack this creature, turn to **212**. If you would rather close the door and walk further up the tunnel, turn to **32**.

61

You are surrounded by a pile of broken bones which you have to brush aside with your sword in order to make a path. You search the cupboards in the room but find only crude bowls, plates and spoons. But under the serving hatch you discover a thin leather case, half a metre long. If you want to open this case, turn to **119**. If you would rather leave it unopened, walk back down the tunnel and turn right at the last junction, turn to **37**.

62

The copper bracelet is a magic healing band. Your wounds are healed and a sudden feeling of strength surges through your body. Regain 4 STAMINA points. If you want to hang the pendant round your neck, turn to **105**. Otherwise, if you have not done so already, you may take a look at the weapons (turn to **206**) or leave the room and walk further up the tunnel (turn to **151**).

63

The Sentinel collapses to the ground in a myriad pieces, broken like a shattered window. If you now want to enter the left-hand runnel, turn to **124**. If you prefer to enter the right-hand tunnel, turn to **38**.

64

The day rolls by without incident until you make out the sound of somebody running towards you. You turn around to see a tall, ugly humanoid whose face is lumpy and beast-like. From its mouth it is drooling spittle all over itself as it strives to catch up with you. Its clothing is primitive, no more than loincloth made of animal skins. It is an Ogre and it is armed with a spear and a heavy club. If you want to stand your ground and fight, turn to **395**. If you prefer to try to outrun the Ogre, turn to **126**.

65

You tap the ground twice with the staff – and as quickly as the chasm had opened up, the ground closes again. The Death Lords look suddenly nervous as you walk towards them with the skull staff in your hand. One of them calls out and they all throw their razor-sharp spheres at you. Roll one die, then add 1 to the number rolled for each of the following pieces of armour you may be wearing or carrying: a shield, a helmet or a breastplate. If the total is 1–4, turn to **285**. If the total is 5 or more, turn to **335**.

66

If you are carrying any of the following items, you have time to grab just one before the advancing Gorgon is upon you. Will you choose:

Garlic?   Turn to **15**

A mirror?   Turn to **231**

A whistle?   Turn to **334**

If you have none of these articles, you will have to attack the Gorgon with your sword after all (turn to **393**).

67

The slime flies past your head, only just missing you. The blind worm starts to writhe around and falls off the box. You seize your opportunity, grab the box and scramble up out of the pit. Back in the tunnel you shake the box but can hear nothing rattling inside it. You lift the lid gently, only to find that all the box contains is a page from a tiny book. You turn the box over and see that the word 'Fire' is scratched on the base. The box is quite large and, if you wish to fit it in your backpack and take it with you, you will have to leave two other items behind (remove them from your *Equipment List)*. After making up your mind about the box, you may now either read the page from the book, turn to **230**) or walk further up the tunnel (turn to **97**).

68

The tunnel is dark and you are forced to use your hands to grope along the floor ahead of you to avoid the chance of falling down an unseen shaft. About twenty metres further ahead, your hand encounters an iron spike that has been driven into the stone floor, beyond the spike, the floor disappears and becomes a total black void. You are fairly sure that the tunnel ends at the far side of the shaft, since you can just make out a wall – a certain dead-end. Just as you are wondering how far down it is to the bottom of the shaft, you hear the unnerving sound of metal grating on stone coming along the tunnel behind you. You feel trapped – perhaps it's the Goblin, but how could he be behind you, since you did not find him in his room? If you want to turn around and crawl back along the tunnel, turn to **114**. If you'd rather attempt to climb down the shaft, turn to **383**.

69

You stride confidently over to the guard. What will you do to get it to open the door?

Offer it 10 Gold Pieces?	Turn to **214**
Tell it that you are the relief guard?	Turn to **385**
Offer it Darkblade Skullbiter's sword?	Turn to **202**

70

Regaining your balance you bend over the sleeping Troglodyte and pick up its throwing dagger and pouch. Inside the pouch you find a piece of slate with the word 'arrow' scratched on it. You put this in your pocket and slip the dagger down the side of your boot. Seeing nothing else of interest, you tiptoe quietly over to the far door (turn to **158**).

71

The giant eagle appears to be completely unperturbed when Zoot fixes a harness and a two-man saddle across its back. When he has finished the job, Zoot turns to you and says, 'Don't even think about offering me payment for this trip. I just want my mother to be avenged, as I am convinced that this terrible plague which is destroying Kaad is of Zagor's doing. Come on, climb aboard!' You do as Zoot asks and, with a flutter of its massive wings, the eagle carries you high into the sky.

Kaad is soon left behind and it becomes just another small feature of the landscape beneath you. The sensation of flying is exhilarating and for a moment you forget the dangerous task that awaits you. Zoot steers the great bird northeastwards, high above the Pagan Plains.

For half an hour you see no other creatures in the sky, but then your luck runs out. Zoot suddenly points towards the distant horizon, where another flying creature is coming into view. If you want to instruct him to land, turn to **240**. If you would rather order him to fly on towards Firetop Mountain, turn to **131**.

In front of you are two servants of Zagor

72

You leap into the bushes, your sword cutting through the air. To your right is Moose and in front of you are the two servants of Zagor: they crouch, daggers drawn, and growl, foamy spittle dripping from their dog-like jaws. Half Dark Elf and half Goblin, Trackers are perfect hunters and messengers. Always armed with a cross-belt of throwing daggers across their chest, they will not usually fight openly unless cornered. Suddenly they throw their daggers at you and Moose and draw their short swords. But you are ready and duck below the flying dagger. Wasting not a second more, you charge at the nearest Tracker.

TRACKER   SKILL 7   STAMINA 6

If you win, turn to **306**.

73

If your current LUCK score is 9 or above, turn to **167**. If it is 8 or less, turn to **320**.

74

Your outstretched hand grasps the door handle at the same moment as three spears thump into your back. You stumble forward, fall against the door and slide down to the floor. Your adventure is over.

75

The key turns in the door and you walk through, with the feeling that you may be nearing the end of your quest (turn to **169**).

76

You look up to see the Pitmaster throwing the rope down into the pit. After retrieving your sword you swarm up the rope and await his judgement. 'You have earned the right to enter the inner sanctum of Firetop Mountain, where the harmony of the spheres aligns itself to Chaos,' the Pitmaster announces solemnly. 'You may now go.'

As you make your way to the far end of the cavern and a new tunnel, you wonder if the Pitmaster knows of your quest. Surely he must be a servant of Zagor? Why didn't he try to kill you? You resist the temptation to look back over your shoulder and enter the tunnel (turn to **337**).

77

With her sails hoisted and trimmed, the boat is quickly underway and the war canoes are soon left far behind.

'No more stops until Kaad,' snarls Lorrie, pulling hard at the helm. Feeling guilty, you sit alone on the rack, watching the vivid landscape speed by. *Test your Luck*. If you are Lucky, turn to **40**. If you are Unlucky, turn to **258**.

78

The garlic fumes activate an ancient spell that, unknown to you, has been cast on the pendant. The pendant changes shape and turns into a stiletto blade which thrusts itself through your backpack and shirt. Its deadly tip pierces your heart. Your adventure is over.

79

You uncover your eyes and see the hideous creature lying in a pool of green slime which oozes from its wounds. Bathed in sweat, you slump against a wall to recover, not daring to take your eyes off the Gorgon and the snakes on her head, which continue to writhe around. A minute or so later, you feel you are ready to move on. If you want to open the new door, turn to **347**. If you would rather look inside the adjoining chamber from where the Gorgon emerged, turn to **209**.

80

Lighting your lantern, you find yourself in a small, empty chamber which has a tunnel leading from its far wall. There appears to be a message on this wall, written in yellow chalk. If you want to read the message, turn to **323**. If you would rather walk straight along the tunnel, turn to **372**.

81

There is just a single sentence on the page; it reads: *The Fire Elemental of Light is numbered 315 and destroys an Earth Elemental of Chaos*. You memorize these words and decide what to do next. If you want to take the dragon's head, turn to **73**. If you would rather leave the room as it is and turn left into the tunnel, turn to **32**.

82

You find a round, polished shield, half buried in the dirt. Take it if you wish and turn to **267**.

83

'Zagor? That was last week's password. Now be off with you or I'll call the guard,' the doorman says angrily. You decide against pushing your luck too far and set off along the tunnel (turn to **304**).

84

You place a Gold Piece on the palm of your hand and shove your arm through the cell bars, urging the Goblin to approach and communicate with you. With Zagor's coins you hope to convince him that you are an ally, a fellow-servant of Zagor. *Test your Luck.* If you are Lucky, turn to **164**. If you are Unlucky, turn to **327**.

85

The Mummies become aware of your presence and shuffle towards you, their arms outstretched. You know that, while they are not savage fighters, they are difficult to defeat since they cannot be properly killed by normal weapons. The only sure way of defeating them is by fire. If you have a lantern, turn to **288**. If you do not have a lantern, turn to **239**.

86

A few hours later it is beginning to get dark and, with Firetop Mountain now plainly visible in the distance, you wonder whether to settle down and sleep out on the open plain or to press on. A group of large boulders, two hundred metres to your left, offer some sort of protection, but you can see nowhere else to take shelter. If you wish to go over to the boulders, turn to **263**. If you would rather walk on in darkness, turn to **357**.

The skeleton's jaw hangs open, as though screaming in agony

87

You enter a derelict room that was once a torture chamber. All manner of instruments of pain are strewn about; branding irons, knives, chains, thumbscrews, ropes, whips and an iron maiden, all long since abandoned, lie covered in dust and cobwebs on the stone floor. In the middle of the chamber you see a rack, the most feared torture instrument known. The skeleton of an unfortunate victim is still tied to the rack; the skeleton's jaw hangs open, as though screaming in agony. On closer inspection you notice a gold ring on one of the fingers of the skeleton. If you wish to take this ring, turn to **5**. If you would rather leave the torture chamber and carry on up the tunnel, turn to **23**.

88

Not waiting to see whether the Chaos Warrior will rise again, you leave the room, slamming the door behind you, and turn right up the tunnel (turn to **151**).

89

You swim to the northern bank of the river and scramble up it, panting in exhaustion. You look back and see the boat drifting off downstream, but no crew members are left alive, just the thrashing waters as more Razorfish swim in to feed. If you wish to rest for a while, turn to **155**. If you would rather set off to the west towards Kaad, turn to **379**.

90

'Correct,' says the Inquisitor. 'You have earned the right to enter the inner sanctum of Firetop Mountain, where the harmony of the spheres aligns itself to Chaos. If you wish, you may avail yourself of my library before you go.'

If you want to peruse some of his books, turn to **18**. If you would rather walk through the cavern and into the tunnel at the far end, turn to **337**.

91

'Good!' says the Troglodyte. 'I'd forgotten about the prize for the runner-up. Is it gold or silver this time?' In order to avoid suspicion, you must give the Troglodyte one item which is made of either gold or silver. If you have such an item to give him, turn to **26**. If you do not have either a gold or a silver item to give away, turn to **122**.

92

You reach down into the compartment until your hand touches a jelly-like substance at the bottom. If you are wearing leather gloves, turn to **178**. If you do not have a pair of gloves on, turn to **377**.

93

The box is empty, apart from a ball of string. You put the string in your backpack and leave the room through the door in the far wall (turn to **121**).

94

The tooth bounces up off the floor and breaks in two; a massive stone humanoid rises up out of the ground between you and the Air Elemental. It is an Earth Elemental that you have summoned. A great battle ensues as the Earth Elemental, its head down, slowly pushes back the raging whirlwind until its evil forces are spent. Quiet suddenly returns to the hall as the wind drops. The Air Elemental is defeated and the Earth Elemental shrinks back into the tooth on the floor.

Zagor looks surprised, then frowns while he concentrates on his next summoning. A fountain of water suddenly spurts out from the base of the steps and takes on the shape of a watery giant. Like a tidal wave it streams down the hall to engulf you. You need to cast another gold tooth on the floor to halt the Water Elemental. If you know which one to use, turn to the paragraph which has the same number as the one on the tooth. If you do not have the right tooth to counter the Water Elemental, turn to **365**.

95

You make a bed out of ivy tendrils, covered with an old sack. After eating some bread and cheese, you close the trapdoor and settle down to sleep. In the pitch-black darkness you can hear scratching sounds as the insects come out of hiding, but soon you are fast asleep. In the morning, you wake to the sound of footsteps crossing the floor above you. You grope slowly for your sword, trying not to make a sound. *Test your Luck*. If you are Lucky, turn to **352**. If you are Unlucky, turn to **370**.

96

The Gorgon catches sight of her own deadly gaze in the mirror and lets out a brutal, ear-piercing scream. Suddenly motionless, she begins to tremble and her scaly skin slowly lightens until it is the colour of sand. In a few seconds she turns to stone, to become a statue in her own lair. You allow yourself a grim smile while wondering what other hideous creatures still lie in wait inside Zagor's mountain labyrinth. If you want to open the door in the far wall, turn to **347**. If you would rather investigate the adjoining chambers from which the Gorgon emerged, turn to **209**.

97

The tunnel continues straight ahead, and you soon arrive at yet another door in the right-hand wall. You press your ear against the door but can hear nothing. If you wish to open the door, turn to **222**. If you would rather walk on, turn to **373**.

98

You snatch up your blanket and wrap it round yourself and the Fire Sprite. An eerie sound comes from under the blanket, as though the Fire Sprite were gasping for air. Suddenly the blanket goes limp and drops to the ground in a smouldering heap; the Fire Sprite has been banished back to the Plane of Fire. After bandaging your wounds, you spend a painful and uncomfortable night, hardly able to sleep at all.

At crack of dawn you set off determinedly towards Firetop Mountain which, in the morning light, appears to rise menacingly out of the plain. With luck, you estimate that you will reach it by midday. Turn to **221**.

99

The Barbarian swings his furs back over his shoulder and faces you, a two-handed battleaxe at the ready; he will be a fierce opponent. The others in the room start to cheer at the prospect of watching a good fight.

BARBARIAN   *SKILL* 10   *STAMINA* 10

If you win, turn to **135**.

100

As soon as the ear-ring is hanging from your ear, it starts to move of its own accord. The metal earwig frees itself from the clasp and wriggles into your ear. Its many legs are as sharp as needles, causing you sudden pain. *Test your Luck.* If you are Lucky, turn to **274**. If you are Unlucky, turn to **299**.

101

Protected by thick silver scales, Razorfish attack by viciously ripping at their victims' flesh with rows of razor-sharp teeth. The river is soon red with the blood of the crew as two fish swim to attack you.

	SKILL	STAMINA
First RAZORFISH	7	8
Second RAZORFISH	7	8

Fight both Razorfish at the same time. Each Attack Round you must choose which assailant you will attack, then fight it as normal – but both Razorfish will make a separate attack on you! You must throw for your Attack Strength in the normal way against the other Razorfish, but you will not wound it, even if your Attack Strength is greater; just consider this as blocking its attack. If its Attack Strength is greater, however, it will wound you in the normal way. If you win, turn to **89**.

Guarding the door is a brutal-looking beast

102

The door opens into a small antechamber, the main feature of which is an incredibly ornate door in the far wall. A huge letter 'Z' stands in relief on the door, which is embossed with gold leaf. Guarding the door is a brutal-looking beast, its outstretched arms resting on the handle of a large, spiked club. The beast has leather crossbelts looped across its hairy torso and sports two spiked shoulder-pads. While its head is wolf-like, it also has horns and is far more gruesome. Will you try to bluff your way past the guard (turn to **69**) or waste no time but attack (turn to **198**)?

103

The Pitmaster raises his arms and points his fingers towards you as you run to attack him; in a cruel voice, he says, 'Time to die!' Wisps of smoke seem to dance on his fingertips as ten tiny red darts that you thought were his nails fly straight towards you. They strike you with devastating force. Your adventure is over.

104

You lower yourself over the edge of the shaft, hanging on to the iron spike. Your feet do not touch solid ground, so you take a deep breath, let go of the iron spike and drop down into the dark depths below. You land heavily on the stone floor, a few metres below, and twist your ankle badly. Deduct 1 point from your SKILL and 1 point from your STAMINA. If you are carrying a lantern, turn to **80**. If you do not have a lantern, turn to **278**.

105

As soon as you place the pendant round your neck, the Chaos Warrior's body starts to twitch. With its head tilted horribly to one side, revealing the gaping wound of your fatal blow, it climbs back to its feet. You tear the pendant from your neck and throw it on the floor, frantically wondering how to deal with the undead warrior. If you want to fight it, turn to **2**. If you would rather make a run for the door and escape up the tunnel, turn to **388**.

106

You walk back to the path with Moose, deep in discussion about Zagor.

'Mission accomplished anyway,' Moose says cheerfully. 'At least Zagor doesn't know you're coming.'

Eventually you shake hands and say goodbye. Moose sets off on the return journey to Anvil, while you follow the path in the opposite direction. Turn to **161**.

107

As soon as you remove the lid, a large snake rears up and tries to bite you with its venomous fangs. *Test Your Luck*. If you are Lucky, turn to **275**. If you are Unlucky, turn to **302**.

108

Resolving not to go down the sewer after all, you now have to decide whether to sit on the oak chair (turn to **269**) or open the door in the far wall (turn to **283**).

109

You walk along the tunnel, following it round a long right-hand bend, until you come to a door in the left-hand wall. You can hear a noise like the flapping of small wings coming from inside. If you want to open the door, turn to **360**. If you would rather walk on, turn to **172**.

110

You snatch up the spear and steady yourself to throw it at the advancing Ogre. Roll two dice. If the total is less than or equal to your SKILL score, turn to **185**. If the total is greater than your SKILL score, turn to **199**.

111

The spear thumps into your back and bowls you over. In seconds the Lizard Men are upon you. 'Keep this intruder alive for another hour in case Zagor asks for a new arm or something,' one of the Lizard Men growls in a deep, gurgling voice.

You are carried off in chains and thrown into a dark cell. Less than thirty minutes later, a white-robed man enters the cell holding a long, sharp knife. He has come to take a part of your body for Zagor. Your adventure is over.

112

The axe thuds into the back of Fyll, who topples over into the river, dead even before he hits the water. The boat sails on, her crew silenced by the unexpected loss of one of their number. *Test your Luck*. If you are Lucky, turn to **40**. If you are Unlucky, turn to **258**.

113

You take the dragons' teeth out of your pocket just before the Air Elemental is upon you. You must activate one immediately! If you know the magic word that releases the magic in these teeth, you may say it now. Will you shout 'Zabaron!' (turn to **344**) or 'Ca-chondo!' (turn to **55**)?

114

Your worst suspicions are confirmed: the tunnel is blocked by a solid iron portcullis which you cannot possibly move. Suddenly the floor beneath you gives way and you fall a few metres on to a stone floor, landing painfully. Deduct 1 point from your STAMINA. You find yourself in a small, dimly lit room, which is bare except for a straw-covered wooden bed and an iron bucket.

115

There is a wooden door in one wall and a small, barred window. Through the bars you observe the smiling face of the Goblin! You are trapped in his cell. You stand up and go across to the door; peering through, you see that the Goblin is standing in his torture chamber; you hadn't spotted this door when you first entered – it was tucked away in a dark corner. The Goblin lopes over to the rack and gleefully starts to get it ready for you. Then it starts to sing, an awful, repetitive chant, gurgled out of key by a sadistic little creature from whom you still hope to escape. But how? You think hard. Will your escape plan make use of:

The bucket?	Turn to **21**
A Gold Piece with the letter 'Z' stamped on it?	Turn to **84**
A silver key?	Turn to **203**
An iron key?	Turn to **363**

115

The Witch is not carrying anything of any interest to you. However, when you look behind the drapes, you find a metal panel with a handle set in the wall, and a slot above it. 'Silver Coins Only' a sign on the wall warns. If you have 2 Silver Pieces to put in the slot, turn to **264** . If you would like to try two other coins, turn to **362**.

116

The boy's face lights up when you give him the wooden brick. He jumps up and runs off, returning in a few minutes with a rather tubby old man who is chewing on a chicken leg; he is wearing a white apron and seems to be a jolly old soul. 'Shop's closed this afternoon,' he says with a smile, 'but seeing as you gave a present to Deep Sea Junior here, I don't mind opening up specially for you.' He opens the door and you follow him into the rather dingy shop; obviously many of the objects have stood here for years, as they are thickly coated with dust. There's a stuffed bear, some juggling clubs, hoops, large vases, shields, lanterns, boxes, carvings, statues, paintings, bottles, urns, jars, books, maps, clocks, wigs, games, boots and hanks and hanks of different-coloured rope.

'Excuse the mess,' says Deep Sea, 'I must get around to clearing the place up one day. But people usually find what they are after in Deep Sea's Store, that they do. The King of String, they call me! Now, how much have you got to spend and what do you want?'

You open Yaztromo's pouch and empty the contents on to the counter top. You count out 15 Gold Pieces, and you decide to keep back five and spend ten. You ask what might be useful for dungeon exploration and Deep Sea replies, 'Here's my list of equipment for that kind of foolhardiness. Everything costs 2 Gold Pieces. Choose what you like.'

He shows you a slate on which the following items are listed in chalk:

Lantern
Rope
Hammer and Iron Spikes
Garlic
Mirror
Axe
Water Bottle
Magnifying Glass
Quill, Ink and Paper
Silver Dagger
Leather Gloves
Healing Balm

You choose five items (make a note of your selection on your *Adventure Sheet*) and hand over 10 Gold Pieces to Deep Sea. He thanks you for your custom and you leave the store with directions on how to find Zoot Zimmer. Turn to **309**.

117

On seeing your blood flow, the Chaos Beast Man froths at the mouth; its body trembles and suddenly starts to expand, bursting its leather crossbelts. It grows another metre in height and its head expands grotesquely: its jaw extends and two tusks sprout forth. You must continue your fight against the warped Beast Man.

MUTANT BEAST LORD   SKILL 14   STAMINA 14

If you win, turn to **331**.

The door opens into a dingy cell

118

The door opens into a dingy cell. Two rats scurry across the dirty, straw-covered floor as you enter. On the far wall you see a thin man wearing red trousers; he is sitting on the floor and his hands are chained to the wall; a bandage covers his eyes. The man panics as he hears your footsteps. He presses himself against the wall and cries, 'No! No more pain! No more pain!' You think you recognize his voice and try to think of his name. Is it Zoot Zimmer (turn to **57**) or Fergus Finn (turn to **287**)?

119

The case opens quite easily, but you find nothing inside. An inscription inside the lid of the case says: 'The giver of sleep to those who never can.' Disappointed at not having found anything useful, you walk back down the tunnel and turn right at the junction. Turn to **37**.

120

An hour or so later, you hear a cry for help coming from a wood in the middle of the scrubland to your right. If you want to investigate, turn to **318**. If you prefer to keep on walking, turn to **250**.

121

The door opens into a short corridor which ends, a few metres ahead, at another wooden door. You listen but hear nothing. You try the handle and it turns, and you walk into a room which is richly decorated. The floor is of polished marble and the walls are painted white, although grown dull and faded over the years. There are four paler square patches, one on each wall, where, you guess, paintings used to hang. There is a door in the far wall which suddenly opens, and a tall, muscular creature with long arms enters the room. It stops in its tracks when it sees you and starts to drool. Its long, tusk-like teeth protrude menacingly from its bottom jaw. Armed with a spiked club, the savage Cave Troll runs forward to attack.

CAVE TROLL   *SKILL* 9   *STAMINA* 9

If you win, turn to **284**.

122

You try to explain that Zagor has taken all the available gold and silver for a new experiment in sorcery.

'I don't believe that for a second,' the Troglodyte sneers. 'Guards! Arrest this impostor!'

You push the Troglodyte out of the way and run out through the door, turning right. The Lizard Men chase after you, their spears raised. The first one into the tunnel hurls his spear after you as you race away. Roll one die. If the number rolled is 1–3, turn to **234**. If the number is 4–6, turn to **111**.

123

Smiling at the old man's audacity, you take a coin from your pocket and spin it towards him. One sinewy hand snatches it out of the air, and he puts it in his mouth to bite down on it. He grunts with satisfaction then screws up his eyes to examine it more closely.

'Is that the letter "Z" I see embossed on this Gold Piece I have here between my fingers?' the hunchback asks slowly. If you choose to reply that it is the letter 'Z', turn to **29**. If you prefer to say that it is the letter N, turn to **255**.

124

You step warily into a torchlit tunnel. In the distance you can see that the tunnel opens out into another cavern in which there are two pits. From where you are standing you cannot see into the pits, but you can hear growling noises coming from one of them. Standing in the middle

of the cavern is a bald man wearing a chainmail coat. You notice that the nails on his hands are all filed to a sharp point and are painted red. 'Enter, stranger,' his calm voice calls out. 'You have chosen the path of the Pits. I am the Pitmaster. You must prove to me that you are worthy of passing through my domain, and only by the skill of your sword shall you do so. Fail, and you shall die. Step forward to ready yourself for the ordeal, your test begins.'

If you want to obey the Pitmaster, turn to **291**. If you would rather attack him, turn to **103**.

125

The room is very small: it contains two stools, a small table on which lie two bowls of steaming soup, a staff and a wicker basket. A small, clawed foot protrudes from one of the bowls of soup, putting off any thoughts you may have had of drinking it. Will you:

Look at the staff?   Turn to **20**

Take the lid off the basket?   Turn to **107**

Leave the room and chase after
    the Death Lords?   Turn to **219**

126

Your legs are fresh and you soon begin to pull away from the tired Ogre. Realizing that he cannot catch you, he stops and hurls his spear at you. Roll one die. If you roll 1–4, turn to **157**. If you roll 5 or 6, turn to **319**.

127

The Inquisitor raises his arms above his head and says in a cold voice, 'You are forbidden entry into the inner sanctum of Firetop Mountain. By the will of my lord and master, the warlock Zagor, for you it is time to die!'

There is a blinding flash and suddenly the floor beneath you opens up and swallows you. You scream as you fall through the black void. Your adventure is over.

128

The Troglodyte hands the Barbarian a small trophy. It is a bust of Zagor! The Barbarian then turns to you and holds out his hand. You give him a golden object, as you deem it unwise to refuse. (Remove the gold article from your *Equipment List.)* Although you are bloated, the eyeballs are still a source of nutrition. Add 1 point to your STAMINA. After drinking a mug of water, you make your excuses and leave the room, turning right into the tunnel (turn to **304**).

129

A search of the Goblins' bodies reveals nothing, other than a silver amulet of a small rat, which is hanging round the neck of one of the Goblins. If you want to place the silver rat round your own neck by its leather cord, turn to **59**. If you would rather leave the silver rat with its owner and make your way back to the path and then head southwards, turn to **238**.

130

The Goblin ducks and the dagger flies past his head. Turn to **184**.

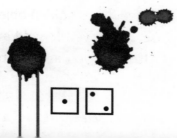

Its bird-like feet are armed with long curved talons

131

As the creature becomes recognizable, a shiver runs down your spine. Cawing and screeching and gliding down on huge leathery wings is a hideous creature with a long sinewy body and a grotesquely over-large head. Its bird-like feet are armed with long curved talons. Looking like a human bat, there is no mistaking the Harpy; it attacks the giant eagle, which is burdened by your weight.

	SKILL	STAMINA
HARPY	7	6
GIANT EAGLE	6	11

Resolve the combat between the two flying creatures. If you have a steel dagger, you may throw it at the Harpy. Roll one die: if you roll 1–3, you will miss; if you roll 4–6, you will hit the Harpy and reduce its STAMINA by 2 points. If the Harpy wins the combat against the giant eagle, you will fall to your death. If the giant eagle wins, turn to **166**.

132

You find yourself in a small kitchen. Everything is filthy: a wooden bowl is stacked high with cracked plates of rotting food; a pot of vile-looking soup bubbles away on top of a wood-fired stove – it smells about as appetizing as the smell of rotten eggs. There are a few jars of herbs on a rack above the stove and a jug of water stands on the floor. You also notice a box of cutlery; sorting through it you find a gold spoon, which you pop into your backpack; then you walk back into the room where the Orc and Dwarf lie motionless. Stepping over their bodies, you leave the room, turning right into the tunnel (turn to **13**).

133

The text on the page is too small to read. If you have a magnifying glass, turn to **81**. If you do not have a magnifying glass, you may either take the dragon's head (turn to **73**) or leave the room and turn left into the tunnel (turn to **32**).

134

The green smoke continues to escape from the canister, but it does not do you any harm; it soon disperses and drifts away. Inside the canister you find a dragon's tooth made of gold and with the number '315' and the symbol of a heart inside a flaming circle stamped on its base. After examining it, you place it carefully in your pocket. Add 1 LUCK point. If you have not done so already, you may now rummage around in the dirt (turn to **242**). Otherwise, you are left with no choice but to go out of this room and walk on to the second door (turn to **56**).

135

You explain to the others that the Barbarian had reneged on the bet. You rummage through the Barbarian's furs and find a cloth pouch. Breaking the string which tied the pouch to his belt, you open it and find a large tooth, made of gold, inside; it has the number '27' stamped on it. Add 1 LUCK point. You put this in your pocket and calmly drink a mug of water to wash away the taste of eyeballs. Although you are feeling bloated, the eyeballs are quite nutritional. Add 1 point to your STAMINA. As the others start to argue over who will have the Barbarian's axe, you slip out of the room and turn right into the tunnel (turn to **304**).

136

As your boat speeds by the Orc, he snarls and hurls a throwing axe at it. Roll two dice. If the total rolled is between 2 and 9, turn to **112**. If the total is 10 or more, turn to **188**.

137

The Lizard Men are tough and skilful fighters. You are lucky that in the narrow tunnel only one can fight you at a time.

	SKILL	STAMINA
First LIZARD MAN	8	8
Second LIZARD MAN	8	7
Third LIZARD MAN	8	6

If you win, you run off up the tunnel before any more Lizard Men appear (turn to **304**).

138

You run over to the door in the far wall while the creature is slithering into the room, but the door is firmly locked. You glance over at the creature and discover that it is not just a giant snake. Standing upright on its huge, coiled tail, you see the large, scaly torso of a fearsome woman, brandishing a silver sword. Small snakes writhe on top of her head in place of hair. Her burning red eyes with their deadly stare slowly search the room for the intruder. You are trapped in the Gorgon's lair. *Test your Luck.* If you are Lucky, turn to **31**. If you are Unlucky, turn to **265**.

139

Remembering Dan's words, you chew the mushroom as quickly as you can, swallowing the last piece just as you feel yourself losing consciousness. You wake up again less than a minute later, feeling perfectly normal once more. Add 1 point to your STAMINA. You stand up, shake yourself and walk on (turn to **373**).

140

The tunnel soon ends at a wooden door which looks as if it was boarded up many years ago. You listen at the door but can hear nothing. You are just on the point of turning around and walking back to the junction when you catch sight of a bottle, tucked away in the corner of the tunnel by the wooden door. On picking it up, you see that it is made of dark-blue glass and is stoppered. There is a metallic object inside which rattles when you handle the bottle. You uncork the bottle, but the metal object will not come out through the narrow neck. If you want to break the bottle, turn to **321**. If you would rather put it back on the floor, walk back past the junction and go on down the tunnel, turn to **281**.

141

As you run to attack him the Inquisitor raises his arms above his head and says in a cold voice, 'Time to die!' There is a blinding flash and suddenly the floor opens beneath you and swallows you up. Your adventure is over.

142

The huge door swings slowly inwards, creaking on its old hinges. You find yourself in a short corridor which leads into a large room. At the end of the corridor you spot a Goblin. At the same moment the Goblin sees you and reaches across to a lever, set in the wall. If you have a throwing dagger tucked down your boot, turn to **34**. If you do not have a throwing dagger, turn to **184**.

143

As night gradually closes in, you find that walking along the path becomes increasingly difficult. Before long you can hardly see the path at all and, as you are still a long way from Stonebridge, it seems pointless to go on any further in virtual darkness. Just as you are wondering where you will find a safe place to sleep, you hear the almost silent flapping of wings above you. Drawing your sword, you strain your eyes towards the dark sky and catch sight of the predatory creature that is swooping down to attack. It is a Vampire Bat and it wants to suck your blood!

VAMPIRE BAT   SKILL 5   STAMINA 4

During this fight you must temporarily reduce your SKILL by 2 because you are fighting at a disadvantage in near darkness. If you win, turn to **350**.

A terrible stench assails you

144

As you open the door, a terrible stench assails you. The door opens into a room with a sunken floor. Looking down, you see three bloated worms, each four metres long, slithering over the carcass of a dead dog. They are yellowish-white and have large, oval, suckered mouths, with which they are blindly trying to grip the dog in order to suck out its juices. There are several rotting carcasses in the pit, and these are the cause of the nauseating stench. As one of the Sucker Worms rolls to one side, you notice an ornately made brass box lying on the floor of the pit. If you want to jump down into the pit to retrieve the box, turn to **7**. If you would rather close the door behind you and carry on up the tunnel, turn to **97**.

145

The pain from the snake bites is so great that you lower you arm momentarily. Aware that the Gorgon is about to strike with her sword, you are unable to resist looking up at her. Turn to **265**.

146

If you want to enter the room, turn to **295**. If you would rather slam the door shut, hurry back along the tunnel and go past the junction, turn to **4**.

147

Your sword slashes through the air in an attempt to fend off the attacking weapons. The sharp noise of steel clashing upon steel rings through the air. For a few moments you manage to hold your own, but the sheer number of blades chopping at you through the air is too great. Silence quickly returns to the room, and the weapons pull themselves from your body and fly back to their racks. Your adventure is over.

148

The key does not fit the lock. A sudden jolting pain shoots up your arm, as if you had been struck by lightning. Deduct 2 points from your STAMINA. Will you now try the iron key (turn to **259**) or the brass key (turn to **75**)?

149

You open the door and walk along a narrow tunnel. It turns briefly to the right and then to the left, where there is a small alcove. Walking on, you arrive at another wooden door with a carved bone handle.

Hearing no sound coming from the other side of the door, you turn the handle. You enter a strange, pear-shaped room with a rough stone floor; there is another door in the far wall and on one side of the room there is a pile of rubble. You suddenly spot a small creature lying asleep on the rubble pile; it has large ears and a long nose, and is wearing only a loincloth. A dagger and a pouch lie by the Troglodyte's head. If you want to tiptoe over to the next door, turn to **330**. If you prefer to sneak up to the Troglodyte and take its dagger and pouch, turn to **45**.

150

You wake up the next morning feeling as though you have slept for a hundred years. Regain 2 STAMINA points. Still yawning, you walk back to the path and continue southwards (turn to **238**).

151

You arrive at a wooden door in the left-hand wall. Listening at the door, you hear the sound of feet shuffling slowly across a stone floor. If you want to open the door, turn to **60**. If you would rather walk on, turn to **32**.

152

The tunnel ends at a solid wooden door with metal hinges; it does not appear to be locked. You listen at the door and hear a noise like that of clinking bones. If you want to open the door, turn to **210**. If you would rather retrace your steps back to the last junction and turn right, turn to **37**.

153

You rummage hastily through your backpack; finding the egg, you throw it at once down the yawning chasm. You hear the sound of it landing, some distance below, but without any magical effect. The island has all but disappeared and you are forced to jump (turn to **46**).

154

As soon as you touch the stone, your hand stiffens and locks up. Try as you may, you cannot move any of your fingers. You have picked up the Gorgon's gallstone, which contains low-strength transmutation properties. Your usual fighting arm is now useless and you must hold any weapons in your other hand. Deduct 2 points from your SKILL. If you have not done so already, you may now smash the brown pot (turn to **397**). Otherwise you have no option but to walk over to the new door in the other room (turn to **347**).

155

Exhausted by your struggles in the river, you decide that a short nap will do you good. Regain 1 STAMINA point. Some time later you awaken with a start as you feel something long and smooth slithering over your body. It is a poisonous snake! *Test your Luck.* If you are Lucky, turn to **223**. If you are Unlucky, turn to **336**.

156

'I thought as much,' the Troglodyte says. 'My friend Zonk was supposed to turn up. No doubt he's fallen asleep somewhere on the way here. This is the only day in the year when we are allowed to enjoy ourselves, and Zonk has to miss it. Well, if you didn't want to enter the competition, what do you want?' If you reply that you have brought a prize for the competition winner, turn to **91**. If you reply that you have been sent to referee the contest, turn to **272**.

157

The spear flies over your head, only just missing you. If you wish to stop and throw it back at the Ogre, turn to **110**. If you would rather keep on running, turn to **353**.

The bell gives out a dull clang

158

The door leads into a tunnel which has been roughly cut into the mountain. It widens out, until you find yourself in a large sand-covered cavern through which a river flows. On the nearside bank of the river a few stumps of wood sticking out of the water look like the remains of a bridge. To their left, an old cracked bell hangs from a post. A sign is nailed to the post but it is too faded to read anything except the word 'Terry'. The river is fast-flowing and looks too deep and treacherous for you to try swimming across, so you decide to ring the bell, hoping to attract a ferryman. The bell gives out a dull clang, and a few moments later a withered old man in a small wooden boat approaches the riverbank.

'Jump in,' he says gruffly. 'Two Gold Zagors to cross, payment in advance.' You assume that inside the mountain Zagor must enforce the use of his gold coins. If you have two Gold Pieces with the letter 'Z' stamped on them and wish to pay the ferryman, turn to **399**. If you do not have the coins or do not wish to pay, turn to **260**.

159

You sense danger. Something is not as it should be. The old man is being too friendly, not the way grumpy old Yaztromo behaves at all. Suddenly you have it! His eyes are green, whereas Yaztromo's eyes are blue! The impostor in front of you must be a doppelganger, a ghost-like assassin sent to slay you. You must pierce its ethereal heart with your sword before its flesh touches yours, or you will be doomed to immaterial existence in a twilight world. To resolve this combat, roll dice as normal, but do not deduct STAMINA points. The winner of an Attack Round rolls both dice again: if a double is rolled, then either the Doppelganger's heart is pierced or it touches your flesh, depending on who won the Attack Round.

DOPPELGANGER   SKILL *9*   STAMINA *0*

If you win, turn to **316**.

160

The Warrior's outstretched hands just fail to catch you as you swerve past him. You slam the door behind you and run up the tunnel (turn to **151**).

161

By midday the sun overhead is shining brightly and it is uncomfortably hot as you walk along the dusty path. You hear the sound of someone whistling, then in the distance you see an old man, leading a donkey. Two large wicker baskets, piled high with mushrooms, are strapped to the donkey's back. As you approach the man, he comes to a halt and, standing boldly in front of his donkey with his arms folded across his chest, he says,

'I'm Dungheap Dan
the mushroom man
I'd rather be a poet
than a man who has to hoe it.'

He smiles and bows, as if waiting for applause. If you want to talk with Dan, turn to **286**. If you would rather ignore him and keep on walking, turn to **237**.

162

You soon arrive at a junction in the tunnel. There is another cave-in in the left-hand tunnel, some thirty metres further on. The roof of the tunnel to your right has also caved in, but there is a new branch in the left-hand wall just before the cave-in. You decide to make a quick right-left turn and make you way up the new branch. The new tunnel soon ends at a sturdy wooden door; you try the handle and it turns. You peer round the door and see a human skeleton lying on the floor of a dust-covered room. There is a fine-looking sword in the skeleton's hand. If you need a sword, turn to **225**. Otherwise, you may either open an old box that is in one corner of the room (turn to **93**) or leave the room through the door in the far wall (turn to **121**).

163

The Death Lords turn and run through an archway at the back of the chamber, screaming at the top of their voices. If you wish to chase after them, turn to **219**. If you would rather enter the side room from which the Goblins had appeared, turn to **125**.

164

The Goblin grunts his acceptance of your proof of loyalty to Zagor, and unbolts the cell door. You nod your head at the Goblin as you calmly walk through the torture chamber, turning right into the tunnel (turn to **23**).

165

There are two small objects inside the skull: one is a tiny dragon's head carved out of bone, no bigger than a button, and the other is a page from a tiny book. If you wish to take the dragon's head, turn to **73**. If you wish to read the page, turn to **133**. If you would rather leave everything where it is, exit the room and turn left into the tunnel, turn to **32**.

166

It is late in the afternoon when Firetop Mountain at last comes into view, its former fiery-red peak now a deathly black. You tell Zoot to make the eagle land as close as possible to the cave entrance which lies at the foot of the south face of the mountain. The giant bird glides down and lands in a clearing. From the ground, Firetop Mountain looks menacing: the steep face in front of you looks as if it has been savaged by the claws of some gargantuan beast. Across the clearing is the dark cave entrance that you hope will lead you to Zagor. Few words are spoken as Zoot holds out his hand to bid you farewell. Soon he is in the air again, turning west for Kaad. You walk up to the cave entrance and peer into the gloom. At the back of the cave there is a tunnel which is lit by burning torches. The walls of the cave are dripping with water and there are stagnant pools on the floor. The air is cold and dank. You hear the sound of tiny feet scurrying across the floor. You take a deep breath, enter the cave and walk on into a tunnel, soon coming to a junction. If you want to turn left here, turn to **281**. If you want to turn right, turn to **140**.

167

The object in your hand is the original lucky charm. It was made by the wizard Probabus who held strange beliefs as to what things in the universe were important and what were unimportant. He held that luck was the all-important force, and that some people and creatures were born with it; he did not believe that good or bad luck happened to people as the result of random occurrences. Probabus liked lucky people and disliked unlucky ones, condemning them as worthless if they had not received their measure of luck. *You* are a lucky person, and Probabus wants you to be rewarded for possessing that quality. The lucky charm detects your high luck factor and rewards you: restore either your SKILL or your STAMINA back to its *Initial* score. You put the lucky charm back inside the skull and leave the room, turning left into the tunnel (turn to **32**).

168

You just manage to clear the skulls and, without stopping to look around, you run on into the new tunnel (turn to **314**).

Two Goblins suddenly appear from a side room

169

You enter a large chamber which is brightly lit by glowing domes on the walls and ceiling. You observe two black-robed men with black skullcaps; between them they are carrying a body towards a marble table, where two men in white robes and white skullcaps are waiting with gleaming knives in their hands. The Death Lords are Zagor's personal physicians. On seeing you, one of the Death Lords raises his knife and calls out. Two Goblins, armed with bows and arrows, suddenly appear from a side room. They both take aim and fire at you. If you are carrying a shield, turn to **340**. If you are not carrying a shield, turn to **189**.

170

The door opens into another tunnel, and after twenty metres you come to a door in the right-hand wall. You can hear great gusts of laughter coming from the other side of the door. You try the handle but it will not turn. If you want to knock on the door, turn to **187**. If you would rather walk on, turn to **304**.

171

You recognize the drawing as that of a Gargoyle, perhaps representing the Gargoyle Constellation of the northern skies. In any case, it does not make much sense to you. You walk around to the other side of the boulder and see the number '92', also painted in the same white paint. Finding nothing else of interest, you set off again towards Firetop Mountain (turn to **64**).

172

Eventually you come to a bend in the tunnel. As you turn the corner, you hear a loud click and the floor gives way beneath you. You fall through a trapdoor on to a bed of iron spikes, some ten metres below. Your adventure is over.

173

As soon as you step among the skulls, they start to close in on you. Their jaws start to click open and shut repeatedly, sending an eerie snapping sound echoing round the room. Suddenly one bites your ankle, tearing away a lump of skin with its sharpened teeth. Another bites your other leg, and the others all try to do likewise. Deduct 2 points from your STAMINA. You kick out at the skulls, sending them flying in all directions. You pull two skulls off your calf and run into the tunnel ahead (turn to **314**).

174

As soon as you touch the hilt of your sword, the Mindbender becomes grim-faced, but then he laughs out loud. If you still intend to strike him with your sword, turn to **232**. Otherwise, if you have them, you can use either your whip (turn to **382**) or some garlic (turn to **224**).

175

Crook slips as he is pulling on the rope to hoist the mainsail and the rope flies out of his hand; the sail comes crashing down on the deck. Another hail of arrows hits the boat; roll one die and reduce the number of the crew remaining by the amount rolled. If any crew are left alive, turn to **292**. If none are left alive, turn to **201**.

176

'I thought as much. You are just another servant of Zagor. You won't get any information out of me. Kill me if you like, but I won't utter another word.'

You try to convince Zoot that you are not his enemy, but he remains completely silent – maybe his injuries have sent him mad. You try to undo his chains, but he waves his arms about wildly to stop you. You realize you cannot help him and leave the room, to walk further up the tunnel (turn to **387**).

177

Without any golden teeth, you are defenceless against the raging wind which envelops you. You are sucked up into the air and thrown against one of the columns. Your head slams against the marble and you lose consciousness. Turn to **208**.

178

Your fingers feel their way through the jelly at the bottom of the compartment and come into contact with a small cylindrical canister. You lift it out and are surprised to see that your glove is now smouldering – the jelly must have been acidic, you deduce, and it was fortunate that you were wearing gloves. Add 1 LUCK point. You see that the canister is made of iron and that the lid will unscrew. You decide to unscrew the top slowly; as you do so, green smoke starts to creep out. If you want to throw the canister back through the hole in the wall, turn to **235**. If you would rather continue unscrewing the top, turn to **134**.

179

The Troglodyte hands you a small trophy: it is a bronze bust of Zagor! You pretend to be grateful. Although you are bloated and revolted at having to eat all those eyeballs, they are still a source of nutrition.

Regain 1 STAMINA point. You turn to the Barbarian and remind him of the bet. He grunts and slaps a cloth purse into your hand. You open it and find in it a large tooth made of gold. It has the number '27' stamped on it. Add 1 LUCK point. After drinking a mug of water, you make your excuses and leave the room, turning right into the tunnel (turn to **304**).

180

You leave the ruined hut and walk over to some rocks, hoping to find a safe place in which to sleep. To reach the rocks, you have to walk through a patch of plants that are red in colour, the same fiery red that made Firetop Mountain famous. On brushing the plants' long leaves with your leg, you become aware of a very sweet smell in the air. You immediately feel relaxed and very tired ... so tired, in fact, that you cannot keep your eyes open a moment longer. You topple to the ground in the middle of the Sleeping Grass, and you fall into a deep sleep full of vivid dreams. *Test your Luck.* If you are Lucky, turn to **150**. If you are Unlucky, turn to **366**.

'Welcome stranger. I am Yaztromo, the wizard you are seeking.'

181

The red-eyed Vampire shrieks at the sight of the garlic and backs against the wall, hissing with fear and hatred. With the garlic held out in front of you, you step slowly into the room and pick up the small box, then you walk backwards out of the room and slam the door behind you. Inside the box you find a quill and an ink bottle full of blood! You decide to abandon your find and walk on up the tunnel (turn to **172**).

182

You soon arrive at the outskirts of the town, and all about you you sense an atmosphere of despair. The occasional person you meet looks either ill or scared, and there is a slight whiff of decay in the air. A cart track runs from the tributary to the town gates, and you see an old man walking along it towards you. He is dressed in long, flowing, scarlet robes and his hair and beard are long and white. From twenty metres away he calls out to you, saying, 'Welcome stranger. I am Yaztromo, the wizard you are seeking, I believe.' On reaching you, he puts out his hand in greeting. His face is suddenly lit up by the sun as the cloud passes by, and his green eyes sparkle. If you wish to shake his hand, turn to **8**. If you prefer not to shake his hand, turn to **159**.

183

The creature suddenly leaps on top of you, scratching and biting viciously. Deduct 1 point from your STAMINA. You manage to shake it off and are about to strike with your sword when suddenly you remember that the Metallix cannot be harmed by any weapons made of metal. You must use the rocks and stones scattered around on the floor of the pit to defeat it.

METALLIX   SKILL *8*   STAMINA *12*

During this combat you must reduce your SKILL temporarily by 2 points, as you cannot use your sword. If you win, turn to **76**.

184

The Goblin hauls on the lever, and a metal plate comes crashing down from the ceiling to block the corridor between you and the Goblin. No amount of pushing can move this barrier and it is far too heavy to lift. You have no option now but to go back down the corridor and turn right into the tunnel (turn to **172**).

185

The spear finds its mark, thumping into the chest of the advancing Ogre, whose face betrays a bewildered look as the large beast sways back and forth, before toppling to the ground. When you have satisfied yourself that the Ogre is dead, you begin a search of its body. A leather pouch on its belt contains a silver key and a lump of cheese. You decide to eat the cheese (regain 1 STAMINA point) and keep the silver key. You wrench the spear free, thinking that it may prove useful later on, and set off once more for Firetop Mountain. Turn to **86**.

186

The tooth bounces up off the floor and breaks in two. A jet of air shoots up from the floor where the tooth hit and starts to spin faster and faster. It increases in size until it develops into the raging whirlwind that is an Air Elemental. As the torrent of water roars down the hall, it is halted by the invisible hand of the Air Elemental. The wall of water climbs up to the ceiling as it battles to push past the raging cyclone that blocks its path. But the Air Elemental is stronger and pushes the wall of water back down the hall until it subsides into a harmless pool. The Water Elemental is defeated, and the Air Elemental shrinks back into the tooth on the floor.

Zagor, now angry, curses and shouts, his good arm

gesticulating madly in the air as he summons yet another Elemental of Chaos. The ground in front of the steps suddenly erupts as boulders, marble and earth rise up and fuse together into a gargantuan stone humanoid – an Earth Elemental. Another dragon's tooth is needed to defeat it. If you have one and know how to use it, turn to the paragraph which has the same number as the one on the tooth. If you do not have the tooth that can defeat the Earth Elemental, turn to **365**.

187

A small hatch slides open in the middle of the door and you see a pair of big eyes staring at you. 'What's the password?' a voice demands. Will you answer:

Zagor?	Turn to **83**
Arrow?	Turn to **204**
Chaos?	Turn to **300**

188

The axe sails over the boat, missing all on board. The crew jeer at the Orc, shaking their fists angrily. Soon the Orc is left far behind as you speed on through the green landscape. *Test your Luck.* If you are Lucky, turn to **40**. If you are Unlucky, turn to **258**.

189

The Goblins are highly skilled archers, and their accuracy is great. Roll one die twice, one for each arrow. If you roll a 1, a 2, or a 3 on either throw, turn to **236**. Otherwise, turn to **358**.

190

If you are at present without a sword, you may take the Goblin's. After a search of the Goblin's pockets reveals nothing more than a stale crust of bread, you decide to search the torture chamber for hidden treasure. Nailed to the underside of a wooden chair you find a leather pouch; it contains a bronze medal with a burning spear embossed on it. You slip this into your pocket and walk out into the tunnel once again and turn right (turn to **23**).

191

The noise you make is enough to awaken the sharp-eared Troglodyte. It leaps up, grabs its dagger and pounces on you.

TROGLODYTE   *SKILL 5*   *STAMINA 4*

If you win, turn to **220**.

192

The ring has lost its charge, and you remain completely visible. You must think of another way to escape from the Mummies. Turn to **85**.

The Warrior raises his sword and lets out a war cry

193

The Fire Sprite is invulnerable to your sword: its blade cuts through the fiery creature, but the flames join up again immediately, and another burning hand grabs your leg. Deduct 3 points from your STAMINA. Reeling around in agony, it dawns on you that you must try to smother the evil fire with your blanket. Turn to **98**.

194

The door handle turns and you walk in on a sight to chill the blood: a fearsome-looking warrior practising his swordplay on a human-shaped block of wood that is suspended from the ceiling. Splinters of wood fly in all directions as the warrior's heavy two-handed sword crunches into the wooden dummy. The warrior is wearing thick metal armour with spiked shoulders; his helmet is horned and covered with demonic symbols – there is no mistaking a Chaos Warrior. On seeing you, the Warrior raises his sword and lets out a war cry.

CHAOS WARRIOR   SKILL 10   STAMINA 10

If you win, turn to **356**.

195

You bring your sword down hard on the Metallix's neck and, although the blade sinks in deep, the strange beast doesn't appear to be harmed in any way – not a drop of blood is drawn. You try to extricate your sword but cannot. Laconically the Metallix raises one arm and slowly pulls your sword out of its neck. It wields the weapon above its head and steps forward to attack. The Metallix cannot be harmed by any weapons made of metal, a fact you suddenly recollect. You will have to do your best by throwing rocks and tones at this adversary. During combat you must temporarily reduce your SKILL by 2 points, as you have lost the use of your sword.

METALLIX   SKILL 8   STAMINA 12

If you win, turn to **76**.

196

The dagger thuds painfully into your left arm, catching you by surprise. Deduct 2 points from your STAMINA. You wrench the dagger out of your arm and charge into the bushes, brandishing your sword in one hand and the dagger in your bloodied left hand. Turn to **72**.

197

Though very weak you know what you have to do, even if the thought of it makes you feel even worse. You comb through the Orc's hairy legs and pick out some fat fleas. You pop them into your mouth one by one until gradually the sickness and fatigue leave you. At last Zagor's curse is lifted. Regain 4 STAMINA points. Feeling fortified, will you now:

Leave the room and turn right into the tunnel?	Turn to **13**
Open the wooden crate?	Turn to **375**
Enter the back room?	Turn to **132**

198

The guard is a Chaos Beast Man, a fanatical fighter which, if in a state of fighting frenzy, can sometimes go berserk and mutate into an even more formidable opponent.

CHAOS BEAST MAN   SKILL 12   STAMINA 13

If you lose more than one Attack Round, turn immediately to 117. If you win the fight without losing more than one Attack Round, turn to **331**.

199

The spear misses the Ogre and lands harmlessly behind it. You hardly have time to draw your sword as the enraged beast lets out a blood-curdling howl and launches a ferocious attack on you with its club.

OGRE   SKILL 8   STAMINA 11

If you win, turn to **248**.

200

You quickly make your escape, leaving the Skeleton Warriors behind in the room. In the light of the tunnel, you see that the 'dragon' is simply carved out of wood that has been painted gold. You put it in your backpack and continue up the tunnel (turn to **373**).

201

Unable to sail the boat on your own, you are left helpless in the middle of the river. You dive off the side of the boat, but three arrows hit you in mid-air. Your body surfaces, to the cheering delight of the Orcs. You are another victim whose blood has helped keep Red River's name notorious.

202

The guard snarls but appears to be interested in the sword. You hold out the weapon and the guard snatches it from your hand. The beast looks closely at the blade and even sniffs it. Satisfied that what it has got is worth having, it takes one of the keys on its belt and unlocks the great door. You waste no time walking through the door (turn to **169**).

203

The key is far too small for the large lock of the cell door. Frantically you try to turn the key in the lock but succeed only in snapping the key in half. You throw the broken key on the floor and wonder what to do next. If you want to use the bucket to escape, turn to **21**. Otherwise, if you have a Gold Piece with the letter 'Z' stamped on it, turn to **84**.

204

The door opens and you are greeted by a small creature with large ears and a long nose; it's another Troglodyte. He is flanked by two Lizard Men guards. He looks you up and down appraisingly and says, 'No one told me any humans were entering the sheep's eye eating competition. Anyway, no matter; follow me.'

If you wish to tell the Troglodyte that there has been some mistake and that you are not entered for the sheep's eye eating competition, turn to **156**. If you prefer to follow the Troglodyte in silence, turn to **43**.

205

Seeking revenge, you raise your sword and attack.

HUNCHBACK   SKILL 6   STAMINA 6

Every time you lose an Attack Round during combat, you must deduct 2 points from your SKILL as a result of being hit by the withering stick, instead of losing STAMINA points. As soon as you win your first Attack Round, turn to **391**.

206

The weapons are all fairly ordinary and are probably those taken from the victims of the Chaos Warrior. There is a leather whip, which you decide to take. Will you now leave the room and walk on up the tunnel (turn to **151**)? Or, if you have not done so already, will you now take a look at the contents of the box (turn to **24**)?

207

The Goblin may be stupid but it is not *that* stupid. It walks over to the cell door and laughs at you. Through the smoke you catch sight of a bamboo tube pointing at you through the bars. You feel a sudden sting on your neck. You have been hit by a poisoned dart from the Goblin's blowpipe. The poison takes effect at once, sending you into a deep coma. When you wake up some time later, you find your hands and feet tied to the rack; you are doomed to a slow and painful death. Your adventure is over.

208

You wake to find yourself strapped down on a marble slab. Your head rings and your vision is blurred and distorted, but you can hear the unmistakable sound of a knife being sharpened. Your adventure is over.

Five skeletons are squabbling over some rat bones

209

Although it has a high ceiling, the chamber is surprisingly small; there is nothing inside it apart from two clay pots, standing in a domed recess in the far wall. A burning candle separates the two pots, filling the recess with a warm glow. You shake the stoppered pots but can hear nothing moving inside the red pot, whereas the brown pot rattles as though a stone were rolling around inside it. If you want to smash open the red pot, turn to **41**. If you would rather smash open the brown pot, turn to **397**.

210

The door opens into a large room which has plainly not been cleaned in years. There is rubbish all over the floor and everything is thick with dust. The smell in the room is unbelievably bad: a mixture of rotten eggs and an Orc's armpit! The room may once have been a dining room, judging by the crockery, cutlery, pots and pans that are strewn all over the place. There is a large table in the middle of the room, around which five seated skeletons are squabbling over some rat bones they have found in a cauldron. Your presence has not yet been detected by them. If you want to enter the room, turn to **296**. If you would rather close the door, walk back to the last junction and turn right, turn to **37**.

211

After sitting down on the bench, you begin to feel relaxed. Your aches and pains are slowly soothed away by the healing properties of the enchanted bench. Regain 2 STAMINA points and 1 SKILL point. With renewed energy and determination, you set off down the tunnel (turn to **162**).

212

The creature is a Plague Bearer and, although it is not strong, a single touch of its hand up on your skin will turn you too into a Plague Bearer, to live for ever in a twilight world of servitude.

PLAGUE BEARER   SKILL 6   STAMINA 4

If you lose even a single Attack Round, you will become a Plague Bearer and your adventure will be over. If you win, turn to **241**.

213

The green tea has a distinctive peppermint flavour, and a warm glow runs through your body. It also has secret healing properties. Regain 2 STAMINA points. After drinking up your tea, you follow Zoot into a courtyard at the back of the house. You watch him crane his neck into the sky and let out a high-pitched whistle. Moments later you make out a speck in the sky; it grows bigger as it glides down effortlessly towards you. It is a huge, beautiful eagle, its feathers magnificent shades of golden brown. With its wings still outstretched, it lands unconcernedly in the courtyard. Turn to **71**.

214

The guard snarls and kicks the Gold Pieces out of your hand. Swinging its spiked club above its head, it lunges forward and attacks you. Turn to **198**.

215

The gold ring is stamped with the number '30' and inscribed with the words 'Seeing Is Believing'. If you want to place the ring on your finger, turn to **384**. If you would rather leave it with the skeleton, you can now either climb up the rope in pursuit of the Goblin (turn to **51**) or leave the room and go further up the tunnel (turn to **23**).

216

In the Wererat's pocket you find a Gold Piece with the letter 'Z' stamped on it. However, there is nothing else of use, so you jump into the boat and row yourself across the river. You are about half-way across when suddenly the boat turns of its own accord and starts to float downriver and no amount of work on the oars by you can alter its course. The river narrows as the walls of the cavern close in. The roof of the cavern lowers until you have to keep below the gunwale of the boat to avoid bumping it. Thankfully, the narrow tunnel soon opens out into another large cavern; this one is filled with giant crystals, all sparkling and glinting in the light of many torches. The boat veers to the left and slides up on to a stony bank. You climb out and stand facing two tunnels. The word 'PITS' is chiselled into the stone above the left-hand tunnel, and the word 'PUZZLES' is chiselled above the right-hand one. Will you now:

Examine the giant crystals?	Turn to **247**
Enter the left-hand tunnel?	Turn to **124**
Enter the right-hand tunnel?	Turn to **38**

217

Gasping for breath, you reach down and pull out the dagger. Forcing it under the warrior's breastplate, you plunge it into his chest, hoping that a pierced heart may halt the undead assassin. Your desperate action is rewarded with success. Once again, the Chaos Warrior falls to the floor. Not waiting to see him rise again, you leave the room, slamming the door behind you, and turn right into the tunnel (turn to **151**).

218

The folded paper is damp with sweat and an unsavoury smell wafts up from it. Holding it gingerly by the corners, you shake out the folds. A pair of blood-red eyes are drawn on the paper. Suddenly they burst into flame and your hands start to tremble uncontrollably. You have been cursed! Deduct 2 points from your SKILL. You drop the paper to the ground and the trembling stops. Moose apologizes at great length, blaming himself for your misfortune.

'Forget it,' you say reassuringly. 'At least Zagor doesn't know I'm coming.' You walk back to the path together and there bid farewell once more; then you set off east alone (turn to **161**).

219

You run through the archway into a circular room with a marble floor. At the back of the room, marble steps lead up to another archway, above which is a single stone with the letter 'Z' embossed on it in gold. But between you and the steps stand the four Death Lords, huddled together on a gold crescent inlaid in the marble floor; they are holding small metal spheres above their heads, as though they are about to throw them at you. They look at you coldly and start to murmur an incantation. The floor starts to tremble as their voices grow louder. Suddenly the floor all round you opens up and you are left teetering on the edge of a deep chasm. Will you try to jump across this chasm (turn to **46**) or use a magic item to halt the earthquake (turn to **354**)?

220

You empty out the Troglodyte's pouch and find a piece of slate with the word 'arrow' scratched on it. You put this in your pocket and slide the throwing dagger down the inside of your boot. Satisfied that there is nothing else of interest in the room, you walk over to the far door. Turn to **158**.

221

As you draw closer to Firetop Mountain, you are amazed at the sight of the once red peak, now coloured a deathly black. When you reach the foot of the mountain at last, you can see how menacing it looks: the steep face looks as if it has been savaged by the claws of some gargantuan beast. You soon find the dark cave entrance that you hope will take you to Zagor. You peer into the gloom and see that the walls are dripping with water which has formed into pools on the stone floor. At the back of the cave is a tunnel, lit by burning torches. The air here is cold and dank and you can hear the sound of tiny feet scurrying across the floor. Taking a last deep breath of fresh air, you step into the cave and walk on into a tunnel, almost at once coming to a junction. If you want to turn left, turn to **281**. If you prefer to turn right, turn to **140**.

There are cobwebs everywhere

222

The door opens into a room which appears to have been long forgotten: the floor is thick with dust and debris, and there are cobwebs everywhere. The only light comes through the open door. At the far end of the room sit two skeletons, slumped in old oak chairs opposite each other and with a table between them. Both are wearing armour and appear to have been playing some kind of board game before meeting sudden death years ago. You notice that the game pieces are all miniature dragons, half of them coloured silver and half coloured gold. If you want to inspect the game more closely, turn to **333**. If you would rather close the door and walk on up the tunnel, turn to **373**.

223

You lie completely motionless while the snake slides across your body and slithers away into the undergrowth. You spring to your feet and set off for Kaad without further delay. Turn to **379**.

224

The Mindbender watches as you hold the garlic out in front of you, then bursts out laughing.

'I'm not one of the Undead,' he says mockingly, 'I am very much alive. But *you* won't be for much longer. The only thing you are good for is as spare parts in our body pool.' A mere flick of his fingers freezes your limbs. You are carried off by Orc Guards to a busy room where Zagor's surgeons set to work on you. Your adventure is over.

225

Before touching the sword, you make sure that it is not wired up to a trap. When you are quite happy that this is not a trap, you take the sword. If you were previously without a sword, regain 2 SKILL points; if; you are already carrying a sword, you now have a spare, which you tuck into your belt. If you wish to open the old box, turn to **93**. If you would rather leave the room through the door in the far wall, turn to **121**.

226

The door opens into a small room which appears to have been an armoury a long time ago: there are three broken swords standing in a rack, some broken spears leaning against the wall in the far corner, and various pieces of dented and rusty armour lying on shelves. The floor is covered with a thick layer of dust and you notice that there are footprints in the dust leading over to the far wall. If you wish to walk over to the far wall yourself, turn to **289**. If you would rather close the door and walk on to the third door, turn to **273**.

227

On seeing you barge into the room, the Orc immediately kicks over the table, sending its stew bowl flying. Grabbing its sword, the Orc leaps at you while the Dwarf runs into the back room.

ORC   *SKILL* 6   *STAMINA* 5

If you win, you take the Orc's sword; however, you hardly have time to catch your breath before the Dwarf runs back into the room, swinging a warhammer.

DWARF   *SKILL* 6   *STAMINA* 4

If you win, turn to **243**.

228

The Witch walks slowly round the glass table and points her crooked right index finger at you. A jagged beam of white light shoots out from it and hits you on the forehead. You are stunned momentarily and find you cannot move; you can only watch helplessly as she picks up another silver headband from the table and places it round your forehead. In seconds your memory is gone, never to return. Your adventure is over.

229

Three glass marbles are all that you find of interest in the pockets of the Hobgoblin: one is purple, one is green and the third is transparent. You put them in your pocket, hoping they may be of use later. The Hobgoblin was also wearing a helmet which looks as if it may fit you. If you wish to try it on, turn to **298**. If you would rather return to the path and continue south, turn to **238**.

230

The text on the page is too small to read. If you have a magnifying glass, turn to **39**. If you do not have a magnifying glass, you will have to forget about the page and set off along the tunnel (turn to **97**).

231

You hurriedly take the mirror out of your backpack and, with eyes tight shut, hold it out in front of you, hoping to reflect the Gorgon's deadly gaze back at her. *Test your Luck.* If you are Lucky, turn to **96**. If you are Unlucky, turn to **256**.

232

'Alas, you have an inferior mind. Your observational powers are useless. All you are good for is to supply spare parts in our body pool,' he says nonchalantly. You draw your sword and make to strike at him but find yourself unable to move; a mere flick of the Mindbender's fingers freezes your limbs. Later you are carried off by Orc Guards to a busy room where Zagor's surgeons set to work on you. Your adventure is over.

233

You say hello to the little boy, but he doesn't look up from his toys. 'If you're looking for Deep Sea, he's not here,' the boy says sulkily, 'but if you give me a wooden brick for my set, I'll go and fetch him!' You are amazed by the boy's cheek and feel like clipping him round the ear. If you have a wooden brick and are willing to give it to the boy, turn to **116**. If you do not have a wooden brick or do not wish to give it to the boy, turn to **44**.

234

The spear flies past your head and clatters to the floor. You run on without stopping until the Lizard Men are well out of sight (turn to **304**).

235

With the canister submerged in the acid jelly, the wisps of green smoke disperse and disappear, causing you no harm. If you have not done so already, you may now rummage around in the dirt (turn to **242**). Otherwise, you have no choice but to leave the room and walk on to the second door (turn to **56**).

236

An arrow strikes you in the throat with deadly accuracy and you topple to the ground. Your last vision is of six heads in a circle above you, looking down with smiling faces. Your adventure is over.

237

Half an hour later you come to a place where the path splits. If you wish to keep walking east towards Firetop Mountain, turn to **19**. If you would rather turn south towards Darkwood Forest and Yaztromo's Tower, turn to **120**.

The massive sail flaps noisily in the wind

238

A brisk three-hour march brings you to the outskirts of Stonebridge. You walk into the village and are met by two Dwarfs. News travels fast in Allansia, for one of them says, 'Welcome, stranger. We have been expecting you.' Seeing your puzzled look, he continues: 'A messenger bird brought us the news from Anvil and we wish to help you so that you can meet Yaztromo. It is your good fortune that you came to visit us, because Yaztromo is not at his tower at present. He has gone to the town of Kaad, which is far to the west of Stonebridge, down the Red River. Plague has broken out there and he has gone to help, but we are not sure if this is of Zagor's doing. We have a fast sailing boat that can get you there in half a day; it is manned and ready to sail immediately. Come now, follow us, we have no time to lose.'

You follow the two Dwarfs through the village to the banks of the Red River, where a strange-looking sailing vessel is moored: it is about ten metres long and is narrow, but with canvassed racks sticking out on both sides. A five-metre pole pokes threateningly out of the bow, doubtless a ramming weapon. The mast is tall and curved, somewhat resembling an enlarged longbow. The massive sails flap noisily in the wind, waiting for someone to harness their power. Nine men stand in line before the boat, their faces brown and lined, as all seasoned sailors' faces are.

The Dwarf points to the men and says, 'These men are good friends of the Dwarfs of Stonebridge. They will take you to Kaad.' Pointing at the shortest man, who is standing at the head of the line, he continues, 'This is Sach, he's in charge. The helmsman's name is Lorrie. The others are Fyll, Eeyun, Stooy, Crook, Maak, Neel and Ndroo.'

You greet the crew and climb aboard. The vessel feels very unstable, being so narrow, and starts to rock from side to side. 'We're out of here!' shouts Lorrie, jumping aboard. The two Dwarfs untie the boat as the rest of the crew also jump on board. They rush about their various tasks: pulling on ropes, balancing the boat, trimming the huge sails. The boat pulls away immediately, ploughing through the water at an alarming rate. Ahead, you notice a rowing boat lying upside-down and bobbing along downstream. An Orc is clinging to the upturned hull. If you want to tell Lorrie to slow the boat in order to pick up the Orc, turn to **398**. If you would rather sail on, turn to **136**.

239

There is nothing you can do to escape the circle of Mummies, so you will have to fight them with your sword. Fight the six Mummies one at a time; each has SKILL 9 and STAMINA 12. If somehow you manage to win, turn to **10**.

240

The big bird glides down to earth and lands on top of a large boulder that stands alone on the open plain. Meanwhile the flying creature passes by overhead, seemingly not interested in what is happening on the ground. After five minutes you judge it safe to continue and recommence your flight to Firetop Mountain. Turn to **166**.

241

You prise the gold tooth out of the dragon's jaw and inspect it closely. It is plain and has no markings. You put it in your pocket and inspect the dirty room. Against one wall stands a small table on which there is a human skull with a candle burning on top of it. You notice that the top of the skull has been cut through. If you wish to lift the top of the skull, turn to **165**. If you would rather leave this room and turn left into the tunnel, turn to **32**.

242

After five minutes spent poking around in the dirt with your sword, you come up with 1 Gold Piece, a tin whistle and an onyx egg. You pack away your findings and decide what to do next. If you have not done so already, you may tug on the chain which is bolted to the wall (turn to **332**). Otherwise, there is nothing for you to do but leave the room and walk to the second door (turn to **56**).

243

If you are suffering from Zagor's Curse of the Demon's Breath, turn to **197**. Otherwise will you:

Leave the room and turn right into the tunnel?	Turn to **13**
Open the wooden crate?	Turn to **375**
Enter the back room?	Turn to **132**

244

There is only half a sentence on the page; it reads: *numbered 94 and destroys an Air Elemental of Chaos.* You memorize the words and decide what next to do. Will you:

Put the copper bracelet on your wrist?	Turn to **62**
Hang the pendant round your neck?	Turn to **105**
Put the bracelet and the pendant in your backpack?	Turn to **313**
Take a look at the weapons, if you have not already done so?	Turn to **206**
Leave the room and walk on up the tunnel?	Turn to **151**

245

You ignore the old man's plea and walk on towards Kaad, leaving him spluttering and cursing behind you. Turn to **271**.

246

The poisonous smoke is lethal. You sink to your knees and soon lose consciousness. Your adventure is over.

247

Walking among the giant crystals, you come across a treasure chest which is filled with gems. If you wish to take a handful of diamonds, turn to **342**. If you wish to leave the treasure, you may enter either the left-hand tunnel (turn to **124**) or the right-hand tunnel (turn to **38**).

248

After the fight you are exhausted, so you sit down on the ground for a few moments to recover. A leather pouch on the Ogre's belt contains a silver key and a lump of cheese. You decide to eat the cheese (regain 1 STAMINA point) and keep the silver key. You also decide to take the Ogre's spear; you haul yourself to your feet and set off again for Firetop Mountain. Turn to **86**.

The mummies begin to climb down from their columns

249

The door opens into another corridor; this, you see, leads into a long, marble-floored hallway which is roughly twice the width of the corridor and is lined with what appear to be statues, three on either side. But in fact the statues are all Mummies, their shrivelled bodies wrapped in stained hessian. You enter the hallway on tiptoe, looking around as you go; at the far end of the hallway there is a door. A clock suddenly chimes and the Mummies all move and begin to climb down from their columns. Not one of them is aware of your presence . . . yet. If you have a Ring of Invisibility, turn to **328**. If you do not have a Ring of Invisibility, turn to **85**.

250

The rest of the day passes without incident and, as the light starts to fade, you begin to think about finding a place to sleep for the night. You know the Dwarf village of Stonebridge is not far away, although you do wonder whether you will be able to reach it before nightfall. Will you find somewhere to sleep while it's still light (turn to **329**) or keep walking towards Stonebridge (turn to **143**)?

251

The slime shoots out and a large gobbet splashes on your cheek: it is acidic and starts to burn. Deduct 1 point from your STAMINA. You wipe the mess off as fast as you can, but the acid continues to burn. If you have a water bottle, turn to **293**. If you do not have a water bottle, turn to **16**.

252

You try to dive to one side, out of the way of the net, but your reactions are too slow. The large net pins you to the ground and, before you can untangle yourself, the point of a blade is being pressed against your throat and a heavy boot is pressing your head to the floor. Out of the corner of your eye you see a Goblin standing over you with an evil grin on its face. Your adventure is over.

253

The portcullis bars your entry to another tunnel; it is too heavy to lift. On the wall on the other side of the portcullis there are two levers, just out of reach. You walk on to the place where the tunnel ends and poke around in the rubble. Here you find a small metal canister which contains a large bronze tooth with the number '280' stamped on it. You put the tooth in your pocket and walk back down the tunnel. Turn to **3**.

254

The Vampire leaps at you with its mouth wide open, intent on sucking your blood.

VAMPIRE   SKILL *10*   STAMINA *15*

You will be able to kill the Vampire only if you are fighting with a silver dagger. If you do not have a silver dagger, you will soon discover that your sword cannot harm it. As soon as you win an Attack Round, you may escape by running out of the room and up the tunnel (turn to **172**). If you win, using the silver dagger, turn to **390**.

255

The old man stares at the coin for a few seconds longer, then looks up and says, 'I don't know of anybody with the initial "N" who coins his own Gold Pieces. But who am I to complain? A Gold Piece is a Gold Piece. Thanks a lot, stranger. I wish you luck. Goodbye.' The old man walks away; but he was a shaman, and wishing you good luck will bring you luck. Regain 2 LUCK points. For a moment you watch him walking slowly down the track, before you turn towards Kaan (turn to **271**).

256

Your shaking hands fail to hold the mirror at the correct angle to reflect the Gorgon's gaze back at her. The towering monster is almost on top of you, and now you will have to defend yourself with your sword (turn to **393**).

257

The Warrior's outstretched hands manage to clutch the collar of your tunic. You feel his vice-like grip on your throat as the undead Warrior blindly tries to strangle you. As you struggle to free yourself, you are forced to drop your sword. If you have a dagger in your boot, turn to **217**. If you do not have one, turn to **311**.

258

Casually looking up into the sky, you see a white dove flying towards the boat. Before it can land, however, a large, jet-black, predatory bird swoops down on the dove, clutching it in its long, sharp talons. The dove flutters its wings in resistance but is carried off by the sleek Blood Hawk to some distant nest to be fed to its young. Turn to **11**.

259

The key does not fit the lock – and a sudden pain shoots up your arm, as if you had been hit by a lightning bolt. Deduct 2 points from your STAMINA. Will you now try the bronze key (turn to **148**) or the brass key (turn to **75**)?

260

The old man becomes angry and steps out of the boat. 'You'll pay for wasting my time!' he says in a voice that sounds almost animal. He starts to expand in size: a bulging torso replaces his hollow chest, his jaw elongates and his bared teeth are sharp and pointed. Thick hair sprouts all over his body. The old man has transformed himself into a Wererat! With claws outstretched he attacks.

WERERAT   *SKILL* 8   *STAMINA* 5

If you win, turn to **216**.

261

You don't manage to jump over all the skulls but land on top of one. It rolls away under your foot and you turn your ankle, losing your balance and falling to the floor, sending skulls flying in all directions. For an instant you are stunned, and you open your eyes to find yourself face to face with a wall of skulls shuffling towards you, their jaws snapping open and shut repeatedly and making an eerie clacking sound which echoes round the room. One suddenly shoots forward and bites painfully into your left ear. Twenty more skulls follow suit, each trying to find an exposed area of flesh to nip. Roll one die and deduct the number rolled from your STAMINA. If you are still alive, you jump up and run into the new tunnel (turn to **314**).

262

You tell the Inquisitor that you are ready. 'Good,' he replies. 'There are two puzzles that you have to solve.' He holds out his arms in front of him and suddenly a sword appears in his right hand and a dagger appears in his left hand. 'The sword and dagger that you see are together worth 300 Copper Pieces. The sword is worth 200 Copper Pieces more than the dagger. How much is the dagger worth?' If you can work out the answer, turn to the paragraph with that number. If you do not know the answer, turn to **127**.

263

With your back pressed firmly against a large boulder, you think about the creatures of the night that stalk the plain. There is some wood close by, enough to build a fire. If you wish to make a fire, turn to **28**. If you would rather go to sleep, turn to **359**.

264

You hear a metallic 'click' and the panel drops down a centimetre. You grip the handle and pull out a metal drawer. Inside the drawer you find a large dragon's tooth made of gold; it has the number '94' scratched on it. Add 1 LUCK point. You leave the chamber with renewed determination and walk back down the tunnel and on past the junction (turn to **4**).

265

The Gorgon casts her gaze down at you and your eyes meet. You are caught by her deadly stare and transfixed by it. Terrible pain creeps through your limbs as they start to stiffen and turn to stone. A fourth statue will soon adorn the Gorgon's lair. Your adventure is over.

266

Your quick thinking saves your life. The blood flows freely from your self-inflicted wound and the poison drips out with it. It may be a painful way to save your life, but it works. Will you now take a look at the staff (turn to **20**) or leave the room and pursue the Death Lords (turn to **219**)?

267

You have to run hard to keep up with Moose. He zigzags through the undergrowth, glancing down at the ground occasionally for prints. All at once he stops and puts his arm up for you to stop running too. You hear a rustle of branches to your left, followed by a piercing howl. Will you charge into the bushes towards the noise (turn to **72**) or stand your ground (turn to **374**)?

268

'I only bet gold against gold,' the Barbarian continues. 'No gold, no bet.' If you have something made of gold that you are willing to bet with, turn to **326**. If you do not have a golden object to bet with, you must tell the Barbarian that you don't want to bet after all (turn to **380**).

269

Sitting down on the smooth, polished chair, you immediately feel very relaxed and drowsy. You cannot stop yourself from falling into a long, deep sleep. You eventually wake up – after how long you don't know – but when you try to stand up you find you cannot move. You start to panic and try frantically to move, but you find it's impossible. You have fallen victim to the Sap Chair. In time you will shrink to a height of no more than ten centimetres and will form part of the ornate detail on the chair. Your adventure is over.

270

Just in time, you dive sideways out of the way of the falling cage. It crashes to the floor with a loud clang. The cage is locked in place and now you cannot move it and reach the panel. You decide there is nothing else for you to do here, so you leave the room and walk down the tunnel and on past the last junction (turn to **4**).

271

Hours later, you arrive at a jetty on the riverbank where a tributary runs into the Red River, and, judging by the number of people milling around, you deduce that you cannot be too far from Kaad. The people are dressed in tattered clothing. They all look downcast with their chins on their chests, and hardly any of them are talking. Most are carrying small bundles and sacks. You decide to approach one of them, a tall man with a black beard, and ask him what is happening. He tells you solemnly that he is waiting for a boat to take him upriver to Silverton, in order to escape the plague which is devastating Kaad. You ask him if he knows the whereabouts of Yaztromo, and he replies that he last saw the wizard, mixing potions to give the sick people, in the town square. The man tells you to follow the narrow tributary north for a short distance, and you will come to Kaad. Turn to **182**.

272

'We already have a referee,' says the Troglodyte with a frown. 'Who sent you?' Unable to think of a name, you decide to make a run for it to the door. You push the Troglodyte out of the way and race out of the door, turning right. The Lizard Men immediately give chase, with their spears raised. The first one in the tunnel hurls his spear after you as you run away. Roll one die. If the number rolled is 1–3, turn to **234**. If the number is 4–6, turn to **111**.

273

The next door in the tunnel is made of solid iron. You press your ear against the cold metal but hear nothing. If you want to open the door, turn to **87**. If you would rather walk further up the tunnel, turn to **23**.

274

You manage to grab the tail of the earwig between your forefinger and thumb just as it is disappearing inside your ear. The tiny needle-like legs dig into your ear as you carefully pull the earwig out. By now it is covered with your blood and wriggles around madly between your finger and thumb. You have saved yourself from a gruesome death by a Brainbiter, one of Zagor's favourite enchanted assassins. You crush the Brainbiter underfoot, then walk to the door before you (turn to **149**).

275

The snake's fangs strike at your armour rather than your exposed flesh. Having failed to bite you, it recoils into its basket, its venom spent. You slam the lid back on the basket to keep the snake inside. Will you now take a look at the staff (turn to **20**) or leave the room and pursue the Death Lords (turn to **219**)?

276

Before you have time to react, the rat's sharp teeth make an incision in your throat. The cut may only be small – but it is big enough to allow Zagor's poison to be injected into you from the rat's teeth. Roll one die and deduct the number rolled from your STAMINA score. Groggy from the poison, you finally manage to tear the rat away from your throat and crush it under the heel of your boot. Cursing the Goblins, you leave the cellar and walk back to the path to continue south (turn to **238**).

It walks slowly towards you, brandishing two shimmering daggers

277

Unknown to you, you have placed a Ring of Undead Calling on your finger. There is a sudden blinding flash, out of which appears a dark figure wearing a long, hooded cloak; it walks slowly towards you, brandishing two shimmering daggers. You catch a glimpse of the creature's face and the sight turns your stomach: the face is drawn and lifeless with decaying skin stretched so tightly across it that it is torn and festering. A maggot suddenly wriggles out of one of the creature's eye sockets and drops to the floor. You have summoned a Death Head, whose sole purpose is to burn your flesh with its white-hot knives.

DEATH HEAD	SKILL 9	STAMINA 9

Unless you have a silver dagger, the Death Head will lose only 1 STAMINA point if it loses an Attack Round. If you win, turn to **35**.

278

You grope around on your hands and knees and discover that you are in a small, stone-walled chamber which you believe is empty. You find a large hole in one of the walls, and you deduce that this must be the entrance to another tunnel. Seeing no sense in staying in the dark chamber, you crawl along the new tunnel (turn to **372**).

279

The rock hits the Metallix's shoulder and it lets out a yelp of pain. If you wish to carry on throwing rocks at the Metallix, turn to **183**. If you prefer to attack it with your sword now, turn to **195**.

280

You throw the dragon's tooth on the floor, but nothing happens. It is made of silver and has no Elemental powers. You are doomed, as Zagor's Elemental bears down on you. Turn to **365**.

281

You soon arrive at a stretch of the tunnel where it curves to the right, and you come across a short, humanoid skeleton propped up in a recess in the wall. The skeleton is wearing leather armour which is dusty and cracked; there are cobwebs over its face and its jaw hangs open. It must have stood here, undisturbed, for years. You walk on round the corner and see three doors in a row along the left-hand wall. All three doors are heavily padlocked and iron bars are bolted across them; they do not appear to have been opened for years. You soon come to a junction. Looking left, you see that in a further ten metres the tunnel ends at a wall. You turn right and come to another junction. If you wish to turn left here, turn to **37**. If you prefer to keep going straight on, turn to **152**.

282

You look around and observe that the Witch is still lying, unconscious, on the floor. Looking back down at the lifeless Dog Beast, you see the sparkling jewel in its headband. If you want to wear the headband, turn to **338**. If you would rather search the chamber, turn to **115**.

*They look as though their faces were set in stone
at the very moment of death*

283

The door opens into a large room with a domed ceiling. The floor is made of polished marble on which three statues stand facing you, each mounted on a marble plinth. The statues are of warriors, and they all look as though their faces were set in stone at the very moment of a horrible death. Their open mouths and screwed-up eyes give the impression of sudden and intense pain. A fourth plinth stands on the floor, but with no statue mounted on it, and there is another door in the wall opposite. As you enter the room to take a closer look at the statues, the door behind you slams shut; at the same time, a wide section of one wall starts to rise up. You can see the tail of a huge snake flick out from under the rising wall and you hear loud hissing sounds. Will you:

Try to open the new door?   Turn to **138**
Try to open the door you
   came through?   Turn to **381**
Get ready to fight?   Turn to **294**

284

A pouch on the Cave Troll's belt holds 3 Copper Pieces, some garlic, a crude metal ear-ring in the shape of an earwig, and a piece of paper with the word 'Leg' written on it. Perhaps the Cave Troll was on a mission to find Zagor a leg for his new body. You may take any or all of the Copper Pieces, the garlic and the piece of paper, and decide what to do with the ear-ring. If you want to wear it, turn to **100**. Otherwise you walk up to the door ahead (turn to **149**).

285

One of the polished steel spheres slices into your forearm and lodges there. Strangely, no blood appears, but, when you try to pull the missile out, you find it impossible to do so. Your vision begins to blur and seconds later you pass out. When you reawaken, you find yourself on a marble table and two Death Lords are hovering above you wielding sharp knives. In lest than an hour Zagor will have a new arm – yours! Your adventure is over.

286

You open your mouth to speak, but Dan immediately interrupts with another rhyme.

> 'Take a mushroom, I won't tell
> When you're ill, it will make you well.'

You realize that talking to Dan would be a waste of time; you accept his gift gratefully, putting the mushroom in your backpack. Dan then sets off with his donkey towards Anvil, leaving you to continue east (turn to **237**).

287

'Do not try to trick me by pretending to be friendly. For a start my name is not Fergus Finn. I was going to tell you my secrets, but I've changed my mind. Kill me if you like, but you won't get another word out of me,' the man declares confidently. You try an assortment of other names and do your best to convince the man that he can trust you, but you get no response: he remains completely silent. You even try to free him from his chains, but he waves his arms about frantically, trying to keep you away. You decide that the poor man has gone mad and decide to leave the room and walk further up the tunnel (turn to **387**).

288

Smashing your lantern with the butt of your sword, you twirl it round your head, hoping to spray the advancing Mummies with burning oil. Roll one die: the number you roll is the number of Mummies you set on fire, their bone-dry bandages igniting like tinder. The remaining Mummies (if there are any) you must fight with your sword. Fight them one at a time; each has SKILL 9 and STAMINA 12. If you win, you know you will have a few minutes to escape before they come back to life. Running towards the door at the end of the hallway, you make your exit (turn to **102**).

289

While you are walking across the dusty floor, the door swings shut behind you. The moment the door closes, some of the broken weapons start to move of their own accord: the swords rise from their rack and the spears move out of the corner. You find yourself surrounded by a circle of hovering weapons. Will you:

Make a run for the door?	Turn to **74**
Fight the weapons?	Turn to **147**
Drop your own sword?	Turn to **348**

290

You scan through a couple of chapters and learn that lizard's blood is the main ingredient in many potions of evil magic. 'Disease', 'Create Zombie', 'Blood Eye' and 'Drain Life' are just a few of the potions that require Vampire's blood. You memorize the information and walk through the cavern and into the tunnel at the far end (turn to **337**).

Drool runs down its bottom jaw as it catches sight of you

291

You tell the Pitmaster that you are ready to fight.

'Good,' he replies. 'There are two fights that you must win.' He leads you over to the smaller of the two pits. Looking down, you see a bloated creature three metres tall and almost two wide; it looks a little like a giant toad. It has green horned skin on its back and a soft yellowish underbelly, covered with red spots. Its head is large and its main feature is a wide mouth with two rows of long, spiked teeth, while two bulbous red eyes protrude above slimy nostrils. It has powerful arms and sharp-clawed hands the size of dragon's feet. Drool runs down its bottom jaw as it catches sight of you, and the creature starts to work itself into a fighting frenzy. You breathe in deeply before jumping into the pit to face the Chaos Slime Beast.

CHAOS SLIME BEAST　　　SKILL *12*　　STAMINA *12*

After each Attack Round, roll one die to determine whether the Slime Beast's acidic drool that it spits at you touches your flesh. On a roll of 1–3 the Slime Beast misses, but a roll of 4–6 means that it hits you and inflicts damage involving the loss of an additional 1 STAMINA point. If you win, turn to **9**.

292

With your help the skeleton crew manage to hoist the sails and the boat is quickly under way, leaving the war canoes far behind.

'Lean out, you lot, and hike! No more stops until Kaad,' snarls Lorrie, pulling hard at the helm. You ignore him, lost in the thought that you were responsible for the death of so many of the crew, and you sit huddled in a cloud of despondency. Nobody speaks for an hour. *Test your Luck*. If you are Lucky, turn to **40**. If you are Unlucky, turn to **258**.

293

You pour water over your burning skin. The water quickly neutralizes the acid and the burning stops. The wounded Sucker Worm is writhing around and flops off the box on to the floor. Seizing your opportunity, you grab the box and scramble up out of the pit. Back in the tunnel, you shake the box but no sound comes from it. Gently you lift the lid and find that the box contains nothing other than a page from a tiny book. You turn the box over and see that the word 'Fire' is scratched on its base. The box is quite large and, if you wish to put it in your backpack and take it with you, you will have to leave two other items behind (remove them from your *Equipment List)*. Now you may either read the page from the book (turn to **230**) or walk further up the tunnel (turn to **97**).

294

Will you fight your new adversary with your eyes open (turn to **265**) or closed (turn to **31**)?

295

As you enter the room, the woman's appearance changes and in front of you now stands a hideous-looking, hunchbacked Witch. Her wiry, bent and hairy fingers end in long, dirty nails. Her eyes are dark and hollow and her clothes are tattered rags. With her illusion dropped she can now concentrate on other types of magic. Turn to **228**.

296

The Skeletons suddenly break off their argument and turn to face the common foe – you! Standing in a line, they attack you one at a time.

	SKILL	STAMINA
First SKELETON	6	5
Second SKELETON	6	4
Third SKELETON	5	5
Fourth SKELETON	5	4
Fifth SKELETON	6	4

If you win, turn to **61**.

297

The rat scurries off with half of the dragon's tooth in its jaws, leaving the Fire Elemental stuck to the floor, flickering harmlessly. Seconds later, the massive Earth Elemental is upon you (turn to **365**).

298

As soon as you put the helmet on your head you get a terrible headache; the pain increases and becomes unbearable. Then you take off the helmet and the pain stops. But something awful has taken place: you can no longer see anything in its real perspective. The Helmet of Confusion has made everything appear distorted, as though you were looking at a convex mirror. Deduct 3 points from your SKILL and 2 points from your LUCK. All the trees and plants that surround you now look short and bulbous. Feeling extraordinarily sad and confused, you return to the path and head south, trying to adjust to the new environment you are seeing (turn to **238**).

299

You try to grab the tail of the earwig as it disappears inside your ear, but you are too slow. The pain increases as it starts to gnaw its way inside your head with its sharp, metal teeth. You have fallen victim to a Brainbiter, one of Zagor's favourite enchanted assassins. Your adventure is over.

300

'Guard! Call the guard! We have an intruder,' shouts the doorman. The door is flung open and three green-skinned Lizard Men barge through the doorway, each wearing spiked leather armour and wielding a spear. You step back, sword drawn. Do you wish to turn and run up the tunnel (turn to **367**) or stand and fight the Lizard Men (turn to **137**)?

301

You explain at great length how you obtained the gold and why you are now on a mission to slay Zagor.

'Why didn't you say so in the first place?' the hunchback retorts.

'You didn't ask,' you reply sarcastically. 'And now, if you don't mind, how about straightening my back?'

'Ah, slight problem there, I'm afraid,' the hunchback mutters, looking a little sheepish. 'I'm not quite up to that sort of hocus-pocus. However, since you are on your way to see Yaztromo, I suggest you get him to straighten you out; he's good at that kind of thing. Or maybe someone in Kaad can fix you up. Now I must be on my way. Sorry about the confusion, but you just can't trust anybody these days. Cheerio and good luck!'

Hardly believing what is happening, you watch the old man shuffle off, leaving you to walk to Kaad, burdened by a not insignificant stoop. But the old man was a shaman, and wishing you good luck will bring you good luck. Regain 2 LUCK points and turn to **271**.

302

The snake's fangs sink deep into your forearm, injecting you with deadly poison. Deduct 2 points from your STAMINA. You make a cut in your arm where the snake bite is and hope that the poison will bleed out. But have you done it quickly enough? Roll one die and keep rolling until you have a total of 20 points. If this takes you 5 rolls or fewer, turn to **266**. If it takes you 6 rolls or more, turn to **378**.

303

You loop the rope round the metal spike and lower yourself slowly down into the inky blackness of the shaft. You reach the bottom, a few metres below, and retrieve your rope. If you are carrying a lantern, turn to **80**. If you do not have a lantern, turn to **278**.

304

The tunnel seems to be never-ending, but finally you arrive at a T-junction. If you want to go to the left, turn to **109**. If you prefer to go right, turn to **349**.

'*Come in and close the door.*'

305

The door opens and you behold a lavishly furnished chamber: the walls are covered with red and purple silk drapes and there are large, brightly coloured cushions lying on the floor. There is an alcove in the far wall out of which a young boy appears, carrying a bowl; he is wearing a silver headband with a large jewel set in the centre. He carries the bowl over to a glass table where a beautiful woman is grinding components with a mortar and pestle. She too is wearing a headband, but hers is made of tiny flowers. Her gossamer-thin robes billow in the draught from the tunnel and she looks up and smiles at you.

'Come in and close the door,' she says in an alluring voice. If you are wearing a gold ring with the words 'Seeing Is Believing' inscribed on it, turn to the paragraph with the number that is the same as that on the ring. If you are not wearing this ring, turn to **146**.

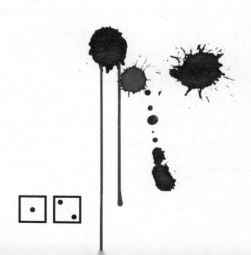

306

You pull your sword free from the Tracker's chest and, looking round, see that Moose has also been victorious, despite a deep gash in his left arm. A search of the Trackers' bodies reveals 6 Gold Pieces, each stamped with the letter 'Z'. You agree to keep three each, and you also take two steel daggers. Not content with emptying pockets, Moose pulls the boots off the Trackers and gives them a shake. A folded piece of brown-stained paper falls to the ground. 'I'm not touching that smelly thing,' laughs Moose. 'If you want it, you can have it.' If you do as Moose suggests, turn to **218**. If you would rather leave the paper on the ground, turn to **106**.

307

The worm slips off the box almost immediately. You seize your opportunity, grab the box and scramble out of the pit. Back in the tunnel, you shake the box but can hear no rattling coming from it. You cautiously lift the lid, only to discover that the box contains nothing more than a page from a tiny book. You turn the box over and see that the word 'Tire' is scratched on its underside. The box is quite large and, if you wish to put it in your backpack and take it with you, you will have to leave two other items behind (cross them off your *Equipment List*). After deciding what to do, you may now either read the page from the book (turn to **230**) or walk further up the tunnel (turn to **97**).

308

You walk to the end of the tunnel and have a poke around in the rubble. You find a small metal canister containing a large bronze tooth with the number '280' stamped on it. You put the tooth in your pocket and walk back down the tunnel (turn to **3**).

309

You find Hobnail Street without much difficulty. Your knock on the door of Number 36 is answered by a tall, thin man whose ears are slightly pointed and who is wearing bright red trousers.

'Hello,' he says in a slow, calm voice. 'My name is Zoot Zimmer and you must be the person who wants to get to Firetop Mountain in a hurry. I can see by your expression that you are wondering how I know that. Well, I heard you talking to Yaztromo – I've got rather good hearing, you see. I'm a Half-Elf. Please come in.'

You follow Zoot into his house, the rooms of which are decorated to resemble a forest. All the walls have trees, bushes, plants, small animals and insects painted all over them from floor to ceiling and all in incredible detail, giving a very realistic effect. 'It's the Elf in me!' laughs Zoot. 'My mother was from the Vale of Willow; she lived with me here until she died of the plague. The decorations made her feel at home. She never did like living in a town.' His face suddenly loses its happiness and a deep frown takes over. 'Would you like some of my special herbal tea before we set off,' Zoot asks.

If you would like some tea to drink, turn to **213**. If you prefer to decline his offer and demand that you set off immediately, turn to **361**.

310

At least one crossbow bolt finds its mark and sinks into your neck. You are dead before you hit the water. Your adventure is over.

311

Gasping for breath, your strength ebbs as the warrior's grip tightens. His own strength is monumental and he lifts you off the ground by your neck. You quickly lose consciousness and death soon follows. Your adventure is over.

312

The crew react by easing the sails and balancing the boat quickly and without undue effort, their long experience making the task look easy. The boat continues its speedy voyage downriver, until at last it glides to a halt at a jetty on the riverbank, where a narrow tributary from the north joins the river. You jump off the boat and thank the crew; as they turn the boat around to sail back upriver, you approach the people standing on the jetty. There are quite a number milling around, most of them poor and dressed in tattered clothing. They are carrying small bundles and sacks, and all appear sad and downcast. You start a conversation with a tall man wearing a black beard and learn that he is waiting for a boat to take him upriver to Silverton, so as to escape the plague which is devastating Kaad. You ask him if he knows the whereabouts of Yaztromo; he replies that he last saw the wizard in the town square, mixing potions to give to sick people. The man tells you that if you follow the narrow tributary north for a short distance, you will come to Kaad. Turn to **182**.

313

If you have any garlic in your backpack, turn to **78**. Otherwise, you may, if you have not already done so, take a look at the weapons (turn to **206**) or leave the room and walk further up the tunnel (turn to **151**).

314

The tunnel ends at a solid wooden door. You try the handle and it turns. The door opens into another small, stone-walled room with a door in the wall opposite. There is a trapdoor in the floor in the middle of the room, which is empty – apart from an ornate oak chair, carved with figures, standing in one corner. Will you:

Open the door opposite?	Turn to **283**
Open the trapdoor?	Turn to **368**
Sit on the oak chair?	Turn to **269**

315

You drop the third golden tooth on the floor and watch it break in two. A jet of flame shoots up from the floor and forms into a huge, fiery humanoid: a Fire Elemental. The Earth Elemental strides down the hall but, strangely, the

Fire Elemental does not move to defend you. As Zagor's Elemental gets closer you start to worry; then you notice that a rat has picked up one half of the dragon's tooth and is on the point of running off with it. Unless both halves are touching the ground, the Elemental cannot be fully released. If you have a throwing dagger, turn to **14**. If you do not have a throwing dagger, turn to **297**.

316

The Doppelganger screams, then disintegrates and drifts away like smoke on the wind. You sheathe your sword and breathe a deep sigh of relief. You walk quickly into town and make straight for the town square; there you find a crowd of people huddled round a lone figure: an old man with long white hair and a white beard and wearing scarlet robes. Yaztromo! You call out his name, and are able to hear his stern reply above the noise of the crowd: 'Who in the world wants me now at a time like this?' You are so reassured by his grumpy tone that it almost brings a smile to your face – except for the fact that he is surrounded by very sick townsfolk. You tell him your name and ask him to spare you a few minutes to help you prepare for your coming ordeal with Zagor.

'Zagor!' he shouts. 'If I hear another person utter that infernal warlock's name once more, I'll turn them into toads!' Yaztromo waves his arms around and indulges in some unwizardly cursing, until finally he calms down and says, 'Now, my good people of Kaad, pass this potion of mine among you and you'll soon be as fit as firefoxes. I must go and see to this young whippersnapper who has just barged in unannounced.'

You walk away from the crowd with Yaztromo, telling him of your quest and asking for his help.

'Well, as you can see, my help is needed here, so I am unable to accompany you. You will have to face Zagor alone and, since he is stronger now than he was ten years ago, you will need to call upon superhuman forces to combat his extraordinary magical powers. You must find the Elementals! Only the Elementals can save you from certain death when facing Zagor. Their material form is that of dragons' teeth cast in gold, each stamped with a number. Each tooth has a special power, but you must learn the magic word that releases their elemental powers. Then it will simply be a matter of throwing the teeth on the floor in order to activate them. Curiously enough, you will find the dragons' teeth inside the labyrinths of Firetop Mountain. It is part of the price for invoking the Raise Dead spell that its user must offer the chance of his own demise. But, as you would expect, Zagor has hidden the dragons' teeth carefully. You'll need at least two – but the more the merrier, as they say.

Now, I must return to my patients.' Yaztromo gives you a hearty slap on the back then returns to the sick people of Kaad. He stops for a moment, looks back at you and says, 'Go and see Zoot Zimmer in Hobnail Street. He's got a giant eagle that could fly you to Firetop Mountain. And it might be worth paying a visit to Deep Sea Dowland's store in Pudding Street. He's got some useful items in there. Here's some gold to spend.' Yaztromo hurls a leather pouch in your direction, then turns to his ailing towns-folk without waiting for you to thank him.

You set off without further delay, heading for Pudding Street. You find Deep Sea's store at the end of a row of shops. Sitting outside the shop is a small boy who is playing with some wooden bricks. If you want to talk to the boy, turn to **233**. If you would rather enter the store without delay, turn to **345**.

317

You examine the breastplate carefully, ever mindful of traps and evil magic, but it looks perfectly normal so you put it on. It is extremely well crafted and will help to protect you. Regain 1 SKILL point and 1 LUCK point. Seeing nothing else of interest, you open the door in the far wall (turn to **170**).

He is being stung by hundreds of red ants

318

You soon come upon a man who is lying, stripped to the waist and staked out on the ground. Somebody has spread honey over his chest and face and he is being stung by hundreds of red ants that are crawling all over him. You hasten to cut him free, then roll him in the dirt to get the ants off him. Although he is in great pain from the angry red bite marks that cover his body, he is not in mortal danger. 'Bandits ambushed me while I was riding along the path. Before taking off with my horse, they decided to make me pay for killing their leader in the fight. Thanks to you, their plan has failed. Here, take this as a reward, stranger; it's a Ring of Invisibility. I suppose I should have used it to hide from the bandits, but it is a very old ring and has only one more charge left. Off you go now. Don't worry about me. As soon as my horse is left alone for even a second by those infernal bandits, he'll come galloping back to me.' After making sure the man is fit enough to be left on his own, you head south along the path (turn to **250**).

319

The Ogre's throw is accurate; the spear thuds into your back, sending you sprawling to the ground in a cloud of dust. The Ogre reaches you quickly and wastes no time in finishing you off, his mission for Zagor completed. Your adventure is over.

320

The object in your hand is the original lucky charm. It was made by the wizard Probabus who held strange ideas as to what things in the universe were important. He believed that luck was the all-important force, and that some people and creatures were born with it; he did not believe that people were lucky or unlucky as the result of random occurrences. Probabus liked lucky people and disliked unlucky ones, considering as worthless anyone who did not possess plenty of good luck . . . You are down on your luck. The lucky charm detects your want of good luck and punishes you. Deduct 2 points from your SKILL and 4 points from your STAMINA. If you are still alive, you throw the lucky charm to the floor, leave the room and turn left into the tunnel (turn to **32**).

321

The noise of breaking glass echoes down the tunnel, and you grip your sword in case the noise attracts the attention of someone you do not want to meet. On the floor you find a small brass egg. You put it in your pocket, then walk back past the junction and march on down the tunnel. Turn to **281**.

322

The text on the page is too small to read. If you have a magnifying glass, turn to **244**. If you do not have a magnifying glass, will you now:

Put the copper bracelet on your wrist?	Turn to **62**
Hang the pendant round your neck?	Turn to **105**
Put the bracelet and pendant in your backpack?	Turn to **313**
Take a look at the weapons, if you have not already done so?	Turn to **206**
Leave the room and walk on up the tunnel?	Turn to **151**

323

The message reads: 'Demon's breath, slow death. Unless you eat some Orc fleas, you will die by this curse! Zagor'. A short blast of warm, stinking air envelops you; this is demon's breath you have inhaled, and it will slowly poison you. From now on, each time you turn to a new paragraph you must reduce your STAMINA by 1 point. If you fail to eat any Orc fleas before your STAMINA is reduced to zero, you will die. You waste no time entering the tunnel (turn to **372**).

324

You try to dive to one side, out of the way of the falling cage, but your reactions are too slow. The cage crushes down on the floor with a loud clang, trapping you inside. You try to lift the cage, but it is firmly locked in place. It won't be long before you are discovered by an Orc guard and are taken in chains to Zagor's surgeons. Your adventure is over.

325

Sleek and protected by thick, silver scales, Razorfish attack viciously by ripping at their victims' flesh with their rows of razor-sharp teeth. The river is soon red with the blood of the crew. The water stirs near you as one of the Razorfish turns to attack you.

RAZORFISH   SKILL 7   STAMINA 8

If you win, turn to **89**.

You are instructed that on the count of three you must start eating, the winner being the contestant to eat the greatest number of eyeballs in five minutes. You pick one up, ready to begin, but the cold and slimy texture of a raw eyeball makes you feel quite sick. Then you hear the countdown: 'One, two, three – go!' You shut your eyes and pop the eyeball in your mouth.

To decide who eats the most eyeballs, roll one die five times for each of the contestants including yourself, adding up the totals for each.

CONTESTANT	1	2	3	4	5	TOTAL
YOU						
BARBARIAN						
CAVEMAN						
TROGLODYTE						

If there is a tie for the highest score, roll the die again between the joint winners until a clear winner is found. If you win the competition, turn to **179**. If the Barbarian either wins the competition or eats more eyeballs than you, turn to **128**. If you don't win the competition but manage to eat more eyeballs than the Barbarian, turn to **351**.

327

The Goblin is not won over by your ruse and hurls a chair at your cell door. You withdraw your arm and step back. A bamboo pipe suddenly appears through the bars and you feel an immediate sharp pain in your neck: you have been hit by a poisoned dart from the Goblin's blowpipe. The poison works instantly. Your adventure is over.

328

You rub the old ring, hoping its magic is still there. *Test your Luck*. If you are Lucky, turn to **346**. If you are Unlucky, turn to **192**.

329

You leave the path and wander into the undergrowth; eventually you come across the ruin of a wooden hut which looks as if it was burnt down years ago. Ivy covers what's left of the walls and floor, and the people who once lived here have long since moved on. You decide to poke around the floor of the hut with your sword. After several stabs into the ivy, you hear a dull 'clunk' as your sword makes contact with something metallic. You cut away the ivy and uncover an iron ring which is attached to a trapdoor. Lifting it up makes a loud creaking noise, and as you peer into the gloom you hear insects and small creatures fluttering and scurrying below. On the top step of the stairs leading down you see a candle and a flint. You soon have the candle lit and climb down into the darkness. You find yourself standing in a small cellar with just enough headroom to stand up in. Cobwebs are everywhere. There are two clay pots on a shelf and a wooden box lies under a rickety old table. Despite the profusion of insect life and small rodents, it seems to be a safe enough place in which to spend the night. Will you:

Go to sleep?	Turn to **95**
Examine the clay pots?	Turn to **386**
Examine the wooden box?	Turn to **33**
Find somewhere else to sleep?	Turn to **180**

330

Stepping as lightly as possible, you cross the room and reach the far door (turn to **158**).

331

The fearsome beast finally slumps to the floor. You are exhausted and covered in sweat after such a gruelling battle. You quickly take the keyring from the guard's belt; there are three keys on it. You have to decide now which key to try in the door. Will you:

Try the iron key?	Turn to **259**
Try the bronze key?	Turn to **148**
Try the brass key?	Turn to **75**

332

The stone to which the chain is attached starts to move. You pull even harder and the stone comes flying out of the wall, almost knocking you off your feet. You inspect the hole and realize that you have opened up a secret compartment. You try to fit your head through the hole in the wall to see inside the compartment, but your head is too big. Will you:

Put your arm into the compartment?	Turn to **92**
Rummage around in the dirt, if you have not done so already?	Turn to **242**

Leave the room and walk on to the
second door? **Turn to 56**

333

As soon as you pick up one of the gold dragons, the Skeletons jolt forward in their chairs, stand up and draw their swords. If you wish to run out of the room with the dragon in your hand, turn to **200**. If you would rather stand and fight, turn to **369**.

334

With trembling hands you take the whistle out of your backpack and blow a few high-pitched notes on it, hoping that some unknown magic will halt the Gorgon. But the whistle is not magical and the Gorgon slithers ever closer towards you. You are suddenly transfixed by fear and stare blankly at the monster towering above you. Turn to **265**.

You are face to face with Zagor himself!

335

The four spheres fly past you, lodging in the wall behind you. As each sphere hits the wall, one of the Death Lords vaporizes, leaving only his robes behind in a crumpled heap on the floor.

Seeing the letter 'Z' above the archway at the top of the steps spurs you into action. You bound up the steps and run through the archway; you now find yourself in a palatial hall: a row of columns runs its length and at the end there are more steps, leading up to a plinth. Seated calmly there on an ornate throne is the most evil-looking man you have ever seen in your life. The skin on his face is drawn taut across his skull and is held by stitches down both sides of his face. His robes are a combination of purple, black and white and a large red 'Z' is emblazoned across his chest. You are face to face with Zagor himself!

'Welcome, fool,' he says slowly and menacingly. 'I have been expecting you, although I didn't think you would get this far. But now your reward is a slow and painful death! It was considerate of you to bring me the last limb I need to rebuild my body. Your left arm looks strong – I'll take it!'

He thrusts his own left arm out of his robes, and you see that it is a skeletal stump. His right arm is also visible and you can see stitches all round his wrist where an outsize hand has been sewn on to a strong arm. This giant hand holds a crystal which sparkles in the yellow light from the domes. Without warning he tosses the crystal into the air and utters some unintelligible words, before catching it again. The air in the hall starts to stir and soon builds to a howling gale. Zagor calmly remains seated on his throne as a whirlwind howls down the hall towards you. Its vaguely human shape means that it can be only one thing: an Air Elemental. But the Elementals that Zagor can summon are the Demon Elementals from the Plane of Chaos. No weapons can affect them. They can be destroyed only by Supreme Elementals from the Plane of Light. Their material forms are golden dragons' teeth. If you have any golden dragons' teeth, turn to **113**. If you do not have any, turn to **177**.

336

Without thinking, you move your hand towards your sword hilt. The snake senses danger and its venomous fangs strike at your hand. The bite is painful – but not as harmful as the poison that now runs through your veins. Deduct 4 points from your STAMINA. You brush the snake off your body and roll away from it as quickly as possible. You jump up to defend yourself, but the snake has slithered away into the undergrowth. Summoning all your reserves of strength, you set off immediately for Kaad. Turn to **379**.

337

The tunnel ends at the solid wall – which, however, slides to one side as you approach it! You enter a large room, and the wall slides back into place behind you. The room is lit by four candles standing at the four corners of a wooden table in the middle of the room. A polished breastplate lies on the table. If you wish to put the breastplate on, turn to **317**. If you would rather open the door in the opposite wall, turn to **170**.

338

The jewel in the headband is filled with dark sorcery. In seconds your memory has vanished, never to return. You wonder why you are standing in the chamber ... but you have no idea. Your adventure is over.

339

You jump back just in time as the heavy net crashes down on top of the skeleton. Looking up, you see a hole in the ceiling. A green, warty face with pointed nose, ears and chin is staring down at you. It's a Goblin and it is angry that it has failed to capture you. The Goblin shakes its fist at you and spits, then disappears. If you want to climb up the rope that is hanging down from the ceiling and attached to the net, and chase after the Goblin, turn to **51**. If you would rather take the skeleton's gold ring, turn to **215**. If you want to leave the room and press on up the tunnel, turn to **23**.

340

You turn your shield in the direction of the Goblins at the very moment when they release their arrows and you hear the missiles thud into the shield. The Goblins run forward to attack you with their clubs, urged on by the Death Lords.

	SKILL	STAMINA
First GOBLIN	5	4
Second GOBLIN	5	5

Fight the Goblins one at a time. If you do not have a sword at the moment, you must temporarily reduce your SKILL by 2 points during this combat. If you win, turn to **163**.

341

You run after Moose, keeping your head down to avoid the many outstretched branches. You catch sight of something sparkling in the bushes. If you want to stop briefly to find out what it is, turn to **82**. If you do not wish to stop, turn to **267**.

342

One of the diamonds in your hand has been coated with a magic potion which reacts when touched by human flesh. If you are wearing leather gloves, turn to **12**. If you are not wearing leather gloves, turn to **42**.

343

The Goblin is *very* stupid and unbolts the cell door. As soon as the handle turns, you charge it, knocking the Goblin over. Springing quickly to its feet, the Goblin draws its sword.

GOBLIN   SKILL 5   STAMINA 5

If you do not have a sword, you must fight the Goblin with your SKILL reduced by 2 points. If you win, turn to **190**.

344

Your knowledge of magic is insufficient to control the power of the Supreme Elementals of Light. Your magic word is wrong! You are suddenly sucked up into the air and thrown against one of the columns. Your head slams against the marble and you lose consciousness. Turn to **208**.

345

You try the door but find it locked; the store is closed. Thinking that you may come back later, you set off to find Zoot Zimmer. Turn to **309**.

The Orc is as ugly and brutal-looking as they come

346

The old ring has just enough magic left in it to make you invisible, but only for a minute or two. While the Mummies are walking around as though exercising their stiff limbs, you escape through the door at the end of the hallway, just as the magic is wearing off (turn to **102**).

347

The door is chained and padlocked; but, using a spear taken from one of the statues, you soon force the lock open. The door looks as if it has been closed for years and you have to tug hard on the handle. Slowly you manage to drag the door open while its rusty hinges creak noisily; beyond, you see a torchlit tunnel. About ten metres ahead there is a door with a barred window in it. You tiptoe quietly along the tunnel and peep through the window.

Sitting at a rough wooden table, an Orc is being served what looks like rat stew by a grisly-looking hunchbacked Dwarf. An ugly purple scar runs down the Dwarf's face from his left eyebrow to his chin. The Orc is as ugly and brutal-looking as they come. You keep watching as the Orc pulls a rat carcass out of the stew with his fingers and eats it, head and all. Under the table you spot a wooden crate. If you wish to open the door and attack the Orc, turn to **227**. If you would rather walk on down the tunnel, turn to **13**.

348

As soon as your sword hits the floor, the jagged weapons encircling you also drop to the floor. You realize it is too risky to pick up your sword again and are forced to leave the room without it. You must reduce your SKILL by 2 points until you find another sword. Lose 1 point from your LUCK. Feeling defenceless, you make your way to the third door (turn to **273**).

349

You walk along the tunnel, following it round a long left-hand bend until you come to a door in the right-hand wall. Listening intently, you hear what sounds like somebody chopping wood. If you want to open the door, turn to **194**. If you would rather walk on, turn to **151**.

350

Still reeling from the unexpected attack, you step warily off the path in search of some cover under which to sleep. You stumble across a fallen tree and decide to sleep beneath its branches. The night passes without incident and, not long after first light, you return to the path and head south (turn to **238**).

351

While the trophy is being handed to the winner, you turn to the Barbarian and ask him to pay up on his bet.

'What bet?' The Barbarian asks, an ugly smile on his face. Will you simply avoid confrontation and leave the room (turn to **6**) or challenge the Barbarian to a fight (turn to **99**)?

352

You feel like a trapped animal, with the blood pumping through your veins, until your hand encounters the reassuring cold steel of your sword. At any moment you expect the trapdoor to be thrown open. You can hear muffled voices, but they do not sound human. The sound of a horn suddenly blasts out and the creatures above you run off. You wait five minutes, before slowly raising the trapdoor. Peering out, you cannot see a living soul. You climb out of the cellar, make your way back to the path and head south (turn to **238**).

353

The Ogre finally gives up its chase and you are able to relax once more and resume a walking pace. Glancing back occasionally to make sure you are not being followed, you press on towards Firetop Mountain (turn to **86**).

354

The small stone island on which you are standing starts to crumble away and grow smaller. You must act quickly – you will have time to try only one item. If you have any of the following objects, will you:

Drop an onyx egg down the chasm?   Turn to **153**
Drop a glass marble down the chasm?   Turn to **394**
Tap the floor with a skull staff?   Turn to **65**

If you do not have any of the articles named above, you will have to jump across the chasm (turn to **46**).

355

Scratched on the hilt of the sword is the name 'Dark-blade Skullbiter'. The name sends a shiver down your spine when you remember that it belonged to one of the fiercest Chaos Champions who ever lived. You wonder why Darkblade's legendary sword is hanging on a Goblin's wall deep inside Firetop Mountain – but, for the time being, your question must remain unanswered. With the Chaos Champion's sword in hand, you squeeze yourself along the narrow tunnel. Turn to **68**.

356

You reason that the room is the living quarters of the Chaos Warrior. There is a straw-covered bed in one corner, a table with a half-eaten bowl of gruel in another corner, and a box of assorted objects on a wall shelf. Numerous weapons are standing in a rack, propped against one of the walls. Will you:

Take a look at the box?	Turn to **24**
Take a look at the weapons?	Turn to **206**
Leave the room and walk on up the tunnel?	Turn to **151**

357

Clouds slowly fill the sky, covering the weak glow from the moon so completely that soon you cannot see your hand in front of you. You have no option but to wrap your blanket round you, hope for the best, and sleep out on the open plain. Turn to **359**.

358

The arrows fly past your head and thump into the door behind you. You run forward to attack the Goblin archers before they have time to reload their bows. The Death Lords scream at them to smash you to the ground with their clubs.

	SKILL	STAMINA
First GOBLIN	5	4
Second GOBLIN	5	5

Fight the Goblins one at a time. If you do not have a sword at the moment, you must temporarily reduce your SKILL by 2 points during this combat. If you win, turn to **163**.

You make out the vague outline of a dark-caped figure

359

Although you sleep uneasily and are awake just after dawn, the night passes without incident. You look eastwards at the imposing sight of Firetop Mountain in the shadow of the rising sun and estimate that you should reach it by midday. Turn to **221**.

360

You enter a dark room which has the smell of death about it. A solitary candle is burning on top of a skull, which stands on a small table against the far wall. There is a small box under the table and next to the table is an open coffin. In the murky shadows in the far corner of the room you make out the vague outline of a dark-caped figure. The cape suddenly flickers, displaying its scarlet lining. The figure slowly steps forward and, as its face comes into the candlelight, you see two long fangs protruding from its upper jaw. It is a Vampire! If you have some garlic, turn to **181**. If you do not have any garlic, you may either fight the Vampire (turn to **254**) or close the door behind you and walk further up the tunnel (turn to **172**).

361

'As you wish,' says Zoot unconcernedly. You follow him outside into a courtyard at the back of the house; there he looks up into the sky and lets out a high-pitched whistle. Moments later, you see a speck in the sky which grows bigger as it glides down effortlessly towards you. It is a huge, beautiful eagle, its feathers magnificent shades of golden brown. With its wings outstretched, it lands in the courtyard. Turn to **71**.

362

You hear a metallic click, followed by a rumbling noise coming from above. You look up – to see an iron cage falling on top of you. Roll two dice. If the total is less than or equal to your SKILL, turn to **270**. If the total is greater than your SKILL, turn to **324**.

363

The key is too big for the keyhole. No matter how hard you push and wiggle the key, it won't fit in the lock. You must think of another way to escape. Deduct 1 point from your LUCK. If you want to use the bucket in your escape, turn to **21**. Otherwise, if you have a Gold Piece with the letter 'Z' stamped on it, turn to **84**.

364

The crossbow bolts fly over your head as you dive into the river. You swim downstream under water until your lungs feel about to burst. When you finally surface, you find yourself in another large cavern; this one is filled with giant crystals, all sparkling and glinting in the light of torches. You swim over to the bank on your left and wade out of the river. You stand facing two tunnels. The word 'PITS' is chiselled into the stone above the left-hand tunnel and the word 'PUZZLES' is chiselled above the right-hand one. Will you:

Examine the giant crystals?	Turn to **247**
Enter the left-hand tunnel?	Turn to **124**
Enter the right-hand tunnel?	Turn to **38**

365

The Elemental crashes down on top of you, then picks you up by your foot and dangles you upside down. The pain in your foot is unbearable and you scream out. For a few seconds you can hear Zagor's evil laughter, before you are hurled against a wall and knocked unconscious. Turn to **208**.

366

You wake up the next morning, feeling as if you have slept for a hundred years. Regain 2 STAMINA points. Sitting up, you are startled to see an ugly, warty-skinned creature in ramshackle armour lying near you; it too is stirring back to life. This is a Hobgoblin and it was going to rob you while you slept, but it became a victim of the Sleeping Grass as well. It sits up and grunts, then suddenly remembers that it was on the point of attacking you. It grabs its spiked club and turns to face you. You must fight the Hobgoblin.

HOBGOBLIN   SKILL 6   STAMINA 7

If you win, turn to **229**.

367

As you run away, the leading Lizard Man hurls his spear after you. Roll one die. If the number rolled is 1–3, turn to **234**. If the number is 4–6, turn to **111**.

368

You raise the iron ring on the trapdoor and lift it up. At once you can hear high-pitched squealing, and a terrible smell wafts up from below. Suddenly a huge rat leaps into the room and you let the trapdoor fall. Roll one die to determine how many Giant Sewer Rats clamber up into the room before the trapdoor slams down. Fight them one at a time. Each Sewer Rat has a SKILL of 5 and a STAMINA of 3. If you win, turn to **108**.

369

In a series of jerky movements the Skeleton Warriors lurch forward together to attack.

	SKILL	STAMINA
First SKELETON WARRIOR	8	6
Second SKELETON WARRIOR	7	6

Each Skeleton Warrior will make a separate attack on you every Attack Round, but you must choose which of the two you will fight. Attack your chosen opponent in the normal way. Roll again against your second opponent. This time, a successful roll means you have defended yourself against its blow, but you do not hurt it. If your Attack Strength is lower, your opponent wounds you as normal. If you win, turn to **58**.

370

Your hand touches your sword but succeeds only in knocking it off the step on which it is lying. It clatters to the ground and you snatch it up quickly. Your pulse races as you stand in the darkness, feeling like a trapped

There are several piles of gold coins on the table

animal. Suddenly the trapdoor above you is thrown open and light pours into the cellar, almost blinding you. You can make out the heads of two creatures above you, partially blocking out the sun. They both start shouting loudly while jabbing their spears down the stairway, but you cannot understand a word they are saying. They are Goblins and you will have to fight them. They descend the stairs into the cellar one at a time, so you are able to fight them separately.

	SKILL	STAMINA
First GOBLIN	5	4
Second GOBLIN	5	5

If you win, turn to **129**.

371

The dagger finds its mark, hitting the Goblin squarely in the chest, and it slumps forward on its face. After retrieving your dagger, you walk down the corridor and enter what appears to be a meeting room. In the centre of the room is a long table surrounded by eight chairs; the walls are lined with shelves full of books, manuscripts, scrolls and maps. There are several piles of gold coins on the table and odd coins lie scattered about the room. A door in the far wall suddenly opens and an old man enters;

372

he is wearing a long purple gown with a raised collar and a purple headband. 'Intruder,' he says grimly, 'you have no right to be here. But if you are smart enough, you may be of use to me. Answer my question and live – fail, and you die. Tell me, how many gold coins are there in this room?'

Look at the illustration and count them up. If you know how many there are, turn to the paragraph with that number. If you get the answer wrong, remember to turn to **232**.

372

The tunnel leads into a candlelit room; it is littered with many skulls, human and animal alike. Two candles, both of which are burning in their brass holders, are mounted on wooden pedestals on either side of the tunnel's entrance. In the opposite wall the tunnel continues into the distance, lit by a long line of torches. You step into the room and, as you do so, the skulls start to shuffle towards you, making the floor by the tunnel's entrance look like a cobbled path. If you try to leap over the skulls, turn to **47**. If you would rather brave walking through them, turn to **173**.

373

The tunnel eventually ends at a T-junction. If you wish to go to the left, turn to **4**. If you wish to go to the right, turn to **48**.

374

A dagger flies out of the bushes, straight at you. If you are holding a shield, turn to **49**. If you do not have a shield, turn to **196**.

375

You soon prise the lid off the crate and find that it is filled with cabbage leaves, most of which are rotten; the smell rising up from the crate is horrible. You rummage distastefully through the leaves and find a small silver bell; you put it in your backpack and consider what to do next. If you want to leave the room and turn right into the tunnel, turn to **13**. If you want to enter the back room and have not done so already, turn to **132**.

376

After picking up and stuffing into your pockets as many Gold Pieces as you can carry, you take a look at the various books, charts and scrolls. Most of them are on the subject of the human and non-human brain. The charts are mainly of Allansia, in particular the areas surrounding Firetop Mountain. The scrolls are written mostly in symbols, but you do find one written in your own language: it is headed *The Elementals*. You read it and learn that, in order to create an Elemental from a golden dragon's tooth, the holder of the dragon's tooth must cast it on the floor and say the word 'Cachondo'. Repeating the word over and over in your mind, you pass through the door from which the Mindbender appeared. Turn to **249**.

377

At first the jelly feels cold and slimy to the touch. But suddenly your hand is gripped by pain as though the flesh were melting. You pull out your arm and are horrified to see that your hand is smoking and blisters are forming. The acid jelly is deadly. Deduct 2 points from your SKILL and 3 points from your STAMINA. You bandage your hand as best as you can and, if you possess Healing Balm, you can restore 1 SKILL point and 2 STAMINA points. If you have not done so already, you may now rummage around in the dirt (turn to **242**). Otherwise, you have no choice but to leave the room and walk on to the second door. Turn to **56**.

378

The poison runs quickly through your veins, long before your remedy can work. You lose consciousness and fall backwards on to the floor. Your adventure is over.

379

Following the track west along the bank of the Red River, you observe a lone figure in the distance walking towards you. Wary of Goblins and other loathsome creatures, you drop your hand to the hilt of your sword. But the figure turns out to be just an old, hunchbacked man, hobbling along slowly and leaning heavily on his crooked stick. Staring at the ground, he takes no notice of you until, drawing level with you, he suddenly turns his head towards you and says with surprising menace, 'Give me a Gold Piece!' If you have a Gold Piece, and want to give it to the old man, turn to **123**. If you do not have a Gold Piece or do not wish to give the old man one, turn to **245**.

380

'Everybody bets on the eyeball game,' the Barbarian says menacingly. 'Maybe you ought not to be here. Guards! Arrest this impostor!'

You push back your chair, get up and race out of the room, turning right into the tunnel. The Lizard Men chase after you, their spears raised. The leading one hurls his spear after you as you run away. Roll one die. If the number rolled is 1–3, turn to **234**. If the number is 4–6, turn to **111**.

381

You run over to the door, only to find that somehow it is securely locked. Looking behind you, you see now that the creature is more than just a giant snake. Standing upright on its huge, coiled tail, you see the large, scaly torso of a fearsome humanoid female, brandishing a silver sword. In place of hair, small snakes are writhing on top of her head. Her burning red eyes with their deadly stare slowly scan the room for the intruder. You are trapped in the Gorgon's lair. *Test your Luck.* If you are Lucky, turn to **31**. If you are Unlucky, turn to **265**.

382

Removing your whip from your belt, you lash out at the Mindbender. Your aim is perfect and the thin leather cord coils round his neck. With a quick jerk, you pull him to the ground. Then you jam a wooden ball in his mouth, cover his head with a cloth bag and bind his arms with the whip to stop him from trying any sorcery. If you wish to search the room, turn to **376**. If you would rather walk through the door from which the Mindbender appeared, turn to **249**.

383

If you are carrying some rope, turn to **303**. If you do not have any rope, turn to **104**.

384

Nervously you slip the ring over your forefinger. Nothing happens – except that a warm glow spreads slowly through your whole body. The strange feeling subsides, and now it is time to decide your next action. If you want to climb up the rope to pursue the Goblin, turn to **51**. If you would rather leave the room and go further up the tunnel, turn to **23**.

385

The guard snarls disdainfully and leaps to attack you, swinging its great spiked club. Turn to **198**.

386

The first pot is empty, but the second contains a large iron key with the number '142' stamped on its barrel.

You decide to keep the key, and you make a mental note of the number. If you have not done so already, you may now examine the wooden box (turn to **33**) or go to sleep (turn to **95**). If you would rather find somewhere else to sleep, turn to **180**.

387

The tunnel ends at a stone wall. You notice some footprints on the floor which all point towards the end wall. You deduce that you are in a secret passageway and that there must be a secret door in the wall. You run your fingers slowly over the wall searching for a tell-tale hairline crack or a hidden latch. Then you discover a loose stone, about half-way down the wall. Carefully pulling the stone out of the wall, you see an iron handle. You twist it to one side and hear a click. Your feeling of triumph is shortlived as a poisoned dart flies from above the handle and pierces your throat. The poison is deadly and acts quickly. Your adventure is over.

388

As you run past the Warrior, he lunges at you and makes a grab for your neck. Roll two dice. If the total is less than or equal to your SKILL, turn to **160**. If the total is greater than your SKILL, turn to **257**.

389

The room is quite small and its floor is covered in bones, debris and dirt. In the far corner you see a chain which is bolted to the wall. Will you:

Rummage around in the dirt?	Turn to **242**
Pull on the chain?	Turn to **332**
Walk on to the second door?	Turn to **56**

390

You watch as the Vampire's body crumbles to dust; in seconds only his cape remains. Suddenly a bat emerges from the cape and flies out of the room. You walk over to the box and find a quill and an ink bottle full of blood inside. You decide to abandon your find and leave the room, turning left into the tunnel (turn to **172**).

391

The hunchback drops his stick, staring almost disbelievingly at the wound on his arm. Then he looks up at you and says, 'Go on then, finish me off!' You sheathe your sword, attempting to convince the old man that you are Zagor's enemy, not his friend. Turn to **301**.

392

The glass ball shatters on the stone floor and you are immediately engulfed in the white smoke. Hacking and coughing, you stagger out of the room, pulling the door shut behind you. Your head spins, and you feel completely disorientated and quite sick. If you have one of Dungheap Dan's mushrooms, turn to **139**. If you do not have a mushroom, turn to **246**.

393

Hampered by having to cover your eyes, you must temporarily reduce your SKILL by 2 while fighting the Gorgon. As you stand your ground before the advancing monstrosity, her frenzied snakes lash out and try to bite you. Roll one die to find out how many snakes bite the hand covering your eyes, then reduce your STAMINA by this number. If you are still alive and the number you rolled is 1–3, turn to **25**. If the number is 4–6, turn to **145**.

394

You rummage through your backpack and find the glass marble; then you throw it down the yawning chasm without delay. You hear it land, some distance below, but without any magical effect resulting. The island has all but disappeared and you are forced to jump (turn to **46**).

395

The Ogre is a ferocious beast and it lets out a bloodcurdling howl as it swings its club at you.

OGRE   SKILL *8*   STAMINA *10*

If you win, turn to **248**.

396

Your blade slices into the huge worm with ease, sending thick yellow slime everywhere. *Test your Luck.* If you are Lucky, turn to **67**. If you are Unlucky, turn to **251**.

A hail of arrows is loosed at your boat

397

You throw the pot on the floor and watch it shatter. A small ball of straw tied with string lies among the broken pieces. You cut the string and open up the straw ball. Hidden in the middle of the straw ball you find a silver ring with the number '69' stamped on it. If you want to put the ring on one of your fingers, turn to **277**. If you would rather leave it on the floor you may now smash the red pot, if you have not done so already (turn to **41**); otherwise you will have to walk across to the new door in the room of statues (turn to **347**).

398

The crew quickly bring down the sails and the boat glides to a halt alongside the upturned rowing boat. Ndroo throws a rope to the Orc, but the Orc turns and dives into the river.

'Ambush!' cries Fyll. Looking behind you, you see two Orc war canoes, that had been hidden beneath the branches of trees along the river, coming towards you. A hail of arrows is loosed at your boat. Roll one die and reduce your crew (ten men, including yourself) by this number. Stooy clutches at an arrow that has gone right through his neck, then gurgles a dying breath and slumps forward on to the deck, his legs twitching in spasms. Ignoring him, the remainder of the crew scrambles to hoist the sails as the war canoes draw closer. *Test your Luck*. If you are Lucky, turn to **77**. If you are Unlucky, turn to **175**.

399

You climb into the boat and the old man rows you slowly across the river. As soon as you get out of the boat on the other side, however, the old man raises his head and howls like an animal and from out of the shadows step four Lizard Men, each armed with a loaded crossbow. Swiftly they take aim and fire as you dive into the murky water. Roll one die. If the number rolled is 1–4, turn to **310**. If the number is 5 or 6, turn to **364**.

400

The Warlock of Firetop Mountain is defeated. Still panting heavily from exhaustion following the battle, you stand over the body of Zagor. Many of his stitches have burst open grotesquely. But at least Allansia is saved! You walk up the steps to Zagor's throne, which is made of solid gold, set with hundreds of jewels. Your fortune is there for the taking. You fill your backpack with treasure and eventually find your way out of the mountain labyrinth.

In just over a day you are back in Anvil, recounting your quest to the cheering villagers. 'Zagor is dead! Long live Allansia!' they all chant. Filled with excitement, they ask you to lead them back to Firetop Mountain so they can witness Zagor's demise for themselves and help themselves to some of his treasure. You finally agree but put a limit of ten on the party to accompany you. The twisting labyrinth of passages appears deserted; Zagor's guards and servants have all fled. When you finally reach Zagor's hall, you find his body still lying, face down, where it had fallen. The villagers crowd round it laughing, commenting and arguing. You walk over and roll the body over with your foot. A sudden gasp comes from the villagers; there is a big smile on Zagor's face and his eyes are wide open, although he is undoubtedly dead. But the thing that worries you most is that his skeletal left arm is missing, and that was the only bit of Zagor that was truly his own. Could that bony stump grow into another incarnation of Zagor? Surely not...

HOW TO FIGHT
THE CREATURES OF
FIRETOP MOUNTAIN

Before embarking on your adventure, you must first determine your own strengths and weaknesses. Use dice to determine your initial scores. On pages 246–247 there is an *Adventure Sheet* which you may use to record details of an adventure. On it you will find boxes for recording your SKILL, STAMINA and LUCK scores.

You are advised either to record your scores on the *Adventure Sheet* in pencil or to make photocopies of the sheet for use in future adventures.

SKILL, STAMINA AND LUCK

To determine your *Initial* SKILL, STAMINA and LUCK scores:

- Roll one die. Add 6 to this number and enter this total in the SKILL box on the *Adventure Sheet*.
- Roll both dice. Add 12 to the number rolled and enter this total in the STAMINA box.
- Roll one die, add 6 to this number and enter this total in the LUCK box.

SKILL reflects your swordsmanship and fighting expertise; the higher the better, STAMINA represents your strength; the higher your STAMINA, the longer you will survive, LUCK represents how lucky a person you are. Luck – and magic – are facts of life in the fantasy world you are about to explore.

SKILL, STAMINA and LUCK scores change constantly during an adventure, so keep an eraser handy. You must keep an accurate record of these scores. But never rub out your *Initial* scores. Although you may receive additional SKILL, STAMINA and LUCK points, these totals may never exceed your *Initial* scores, except on very rare occasions, when instructed on a particular page.

BATTLES

You will often come across pages in the book which instruct you to fight a creature of some sort. An option to flee may be given, but if not – or if you choose to attack the creature anyway – you must resolve the battle as described below.

First record the creature's SKILL and STAMINA scores in the first vacant Monster Encounter Box on your *Adventure Sheet*. The scores for each creature are given in the book each time you have an encounter.

The sequence of combat is then:

1. Roll both dice once for the creature. Add its SKILL score. This total is the creature's Attack Strength.

2. Roll both dice once for yourself. Add the number rolled to your current SKILL score. This total is your Attack Strength.

3. If your Attack Strength is higher than that of the creature, you have wounded it. Proceed to step 4. If the creature's Attack Strength is higher than yours, it has wounded you. Proceed to step 5. If both Attack Strength totals are the same, you have avoided each other's blows – start the next Attack Round from step 1 above.

4. You have wounded the creature, so subtract 2 points from its STAMINA score. You may use your LUCK here to do additional damage (see over).

5. The creature has wounded you, so subtract 2 points from your own STAMINA score. Again, you may use LUCK at this stage (see over).

6. Make the appropriate adjustments to either the creature's or your own STAMINA scores (and your LUCK score if you used LUCK – see over).

7. Begin the next Attack Round by returning to your current SKILL score and repeating steps 1–6. This sequence continues until the STAMINA score of either you or the creature you are fighting has been reduced to zero (death).

FIGHTING MORE THAN ONE CREATURE

If you come across more than one creature in a particular encounter, the instructions on that page will tell you how to handle the battle. Sometimes you will treat them as a single monster; sometimes you will fight each one in turn.

LUCK

At various times during your adventure, either in battles or when you come across situations in which you could be either lucky or unlucky (details of these are given on the pages themselves), you may call on your LUCK to make the outcome more favourable. But beware! Using LUCK is a risky business, and if you are *un*lucky, the results could be disastrous.

The procedure for using your LUCK is as follows: roll two dice. If the number rolled is equal to or less than your current LUCK score, you have been lucky and the result will go in your favour. If the number rolled is higher than your current LUCK score, you have been unlucky and you will be penalized.

This procedure is known as *Testing your Luck*. Each time you *Test your Luck,* you must subtract one point from your current LUCK score. Thus you will soon realize that the more you rely on your LUCK, the more risky this will become.

Using Luck in Battles

On certain pages of the book you will be told to *Test your Luck* and will be told the consequences of your being lucky or unlucky. However, in battles, you always have the option of using your LUCK either to inflict a more serious wound on a creature you have just wounded, or to minimize the effects of a wound the creature has just inflicted on you.

If you have just wounded the creature, you may *Test your Luck* as described above. If you are Lucky, you have inflicted a severe wound and may subtract an extra 2 points from the creature's STAMINA score. However, if you are Unlucky, the wound was a mere graze and you must restore 1 point to the creature's STAMINA (i.e. instead of scoring the normal 2 points of damage, you have now scored only 1).

If the creature has just wounded you, you may *Test your*

Luck to try to minimize the wound. If you are Lucky, you have managed to avoid the full damage of the blow. Restore 1 point of STAMINA (i.e. instead of doing 2 points of damage it has done only 1). If you are Unlucky, you have taken a more serious blow. Subtract 1 extra STAMINA point.

Remember that you must subtract 1 point from your LUCK score every time you *Test your Luck.*

RESTORING SKILL, STAMINA AND LUCK

Skill

Your SKILL score will not change much during your adventure. Occasionally, a paragraph may give instructions to increase or decrease your SKILL score. A Magic Weapon may increase your SKILL – but remember that only one weapon can be used at a time! You cannot claim 2 SKILL bonuses for carrying 2 Magic Swords. Your SKILL score can never exceed its *Initial* value unless you are specifically instructed otherwise.

Stamina

Your STAMINA score will change a lot during your adventure as you fight monsters and undertake arduous tasks. As you near your goal, your STAMINA level may become dangerously low and battles may be particularly risky, so be careful!

Unlike other Fighting Fantasy Gamebooks, in this adventure you do not begin with any Provisions. However, during the course of the adventure, you will have opportunities to regain STAMINA points in various ways.

Remember also that your STAMINA score may never exceed its *Initial* value unless you are instructed to the contrary in a specific paragraph.

Luck

Additions to your LUCK score are awarded during the adventure when you have been particularly lucky Details are given in the paragraphs of the book. Remember that, as with SKILL and STAMINA, your LUCK score may never exceed its *Initial* value unless you are specifically instructed otherwise.

EQUIPMENT

You start your adventure with the basic tools of your trade: a fine sword; clothes suitable for travelling; a backpack to hold any treasure you may come across; and a lantern to light your way.

ADVENTURE SHEET

SKILL		STAMINA		LUCK	

ITEMS & EQUIPMENT:

MAGIC ITEMS:

GOLD PIECES:

TREASURE:

WEAPONS:

ARMOUR:

ENEMY ENCOUNTER SHEET

| SKILL ☐ | SKILL ☐ | SKILL ☐ | SKILL ☐ |
| STAMINA ☐ | STAMINA ☐ | STAMINA ☐ | STAMINA ☐ |

| SKILL ☐ | SKILL ☐ | SKILL ☐ | SKILL ☐ |
| STAMINA ☐ | STAMINA ☐ | STAMINA ☐ | STAMINA ☐ |

| SKILL ☐ | SKILL ☐ | SKILL ☐ | SKILL ☐ |
| STAMINA ☐ | STAMINA ☐ | STAMINA ☐ | STAMINA ☐ |

| SKILL ☐ | SKILL ☐ | SKILL ☐ | SKILL ☐ |
| STAMINA ☐ | STAMINA ☐ | STAMINA ☐ | STAMINA ☐ |

| SKILL ☐ | SKILL ☐ | SKILL ☐ | SKILL ☐ |
| STAMINA ☐ | STAMINA ☐ | STAMINA ☐ | STAMINA ☐ |

| SKILL ☐ | SKILL ☐ | SKILL ☐ | SKILL ☐ |
| STAMINA ☐ | STAMINA ☐ | STAMINA ☐ | STAMINA ☐ |

ADVENTURE SHEET

SKILL	STAMINA	LUCK

ITEMS & EQUIPMENT:

MAGIC ITEMS:

GOLD PIECES:

TREASURE:

WEAPONS:

ARMOUR:

ENEMY ENCOUNTER SHEET

SKILL ☐
STAMINA ☐

SKILL ☐
STAMINA ☐

SKILL ☐
STAMINA ☐

SKILL ☐
STAMINA ☐

SKILL ☐
STAMINA ☐

SKILL ☐
STAMINA ☐

SKILL ☐
STAMINA ☐

SKILL ☐
STAMINA ☐

SKILL ☐
STAMINA ☐

SKILL ☐
STAMINA ☐

SKILL ☐
STAMINA ☐

SKILL ☐
STAMINA ☐

SKILL ☐
STAMINA ☐

SKILL ☐
STAMINA ☐

SKILL ☐
STAMINA ☐

SKILL ☐
STAMINA ☐

SKILL ☐
STAMINA ☐

SKILL ☐
STAMINA ☐

SKILL ☐
STAMINA ☐

SKILL ☐
STAMINA ☐

SKILL ☐
STAMINA ☐

SKILL ☐
STAMINA ☐

SKILL ☐
STAMINA ☐

SKILL ☐
STAMINA ☐

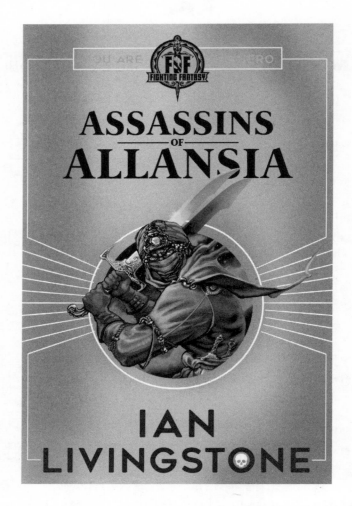

ASSASSINS
—OF—
ALLANSIA

IAN
LIVINGSTONE

After accepting a challenge to survive on Snake Island, a
nightmare unfolds when a bounty is placed on your head.
Beware the ruthless assassins hell bent on hunting you down
– but who are they? Where are they? Trust no-one...

YOU ARE THE HERO

FIGHTING FANTASY

THE
PORT
OF
PERIL

IAN
LIVINGSTONE

Are YOU brave enough to face the savage demons of the underworld...?

Evil stalks the land, as undead hordes rise from their graves to terrorize the living. Embark on an epic quest from Moonstone Hills to the shadowy streets of Port Blacksand to the depths of Darkwood Forest, and ultimately face your worst nightmare...

YOU ARE THE HERO

FIGHTING FANTASY

THE
WARLOCK OF
FIRETOP
MOUNTAIN

STEVE JACKSON
IAN LIVINGSTONE

Are YOU brave enough to take on the monsters and the
magic of Firetop Mountain?

The powerful warlock Zagor must be slain – but first you'll
need to make it through the caverns of his mountain
stronghold. Many adventurers before you have taken a
wrong turn in the maze and perished at the hands and claws
of the Warlock's gruesome servants…

Are YOU brave enough to enter the trap-filled lair of the
sorcerer Balthus Dire...?

You are a fearless young wizard, armed with magic spells -
the last hope to defeat the dread warlord Balthus Dire whose
sorcery threatens the land. You must enter his forbidden
citadel and take on his monstrous minions, or perish in the
process...

YOU ARE [FIGHTING FANTASY] THE HERO

COLLECT THEM ALL, BRAVE ADVENTURER!

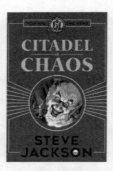

APPOINTMENT WITH
F.E.A.R.

**STEVE
JACKSON**

**ISLAND
LIZARD
KING**

**IAN
LIVINGSTONE**

SORCERY!
THE
SHAMUTANTI
HILLS

**STEVE
JACKSON**

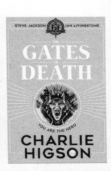

THE
**GATES
DEATH**

**CHARLIE
HIGSON**

CAVERNS
**SNOW
WITCH**

**IAN
LIVINGSTONE**

SORCERY!
PART THREE
CITYPORT OF TRAPS

**STEVE
JACKSON**

**ASSASSINS OF
ALLANSIA**

IAN
LIVINGSTONE

**DEATHTRAP
DUNGEON**

**IAN
LIVINGSTONE**

RETURN TO
**FIRETOP
MOUNTAIN**

**IAN
LIVINGSTONE**

CRYSTAL OF
STORMS

RHIANNA
PRATCHETT